The Farm

by B. West

DORRANCE
PUBLISHING CO
EST. 1920
PITTSBURGH, PENNSYLVANIA 15238

Dorrance Publishing Co
585 Alpha Drive
Suite 103
Pittsburgh, PA 15238
Visit our website at *www. dorrancebookstore.com*

ISBN: 978-1-6470-2307-2
eISBN: 978-1-6470-2827-5

The Farm

Dedication

This book is dedicated to my husband Jim and our newly extended family, on the other side, that continues to grow

THE WESTONS loved their farm where they raised their children and now grandchildren, and they loved their life. Nothing could prepare them for the sudden loss of Jack, the family's rock, and for the immense grief they all felt until he made his appearance from the other side.

It was twenty days after Jack's passing when he first came through to his daughter Lauren and made contact with her. His wife Ellie saw him a few days later in the family room TV silently staring back at her. He had been trying to make contact with her but found that to be more challenging. Lauren was epileptic and took anti-seizure medication that slowed her brain down, and Ellie thought that was how Jack was able to contact her so easily.

The next few months would bring many surprises and heartache while communicating with Jack. He befriends another spirit he meets on their beloved farm who was murdered 170 years ago by his own parents, who ran an unsavory business. Once Jack has Mathew's trust then all the other spirits come forward and want to tell the Westons about all of the terrible events that happened out at the farm and about the brutality of the previous owners so long ago.

Most of the victims were young children, and as many as five thousand perished there at the hands of the runners of the child sex trafficking operation that started in 1813 and operated for almost forty years. They had been waiting so long to tell their stories to the living so that they could move on, and they were entrusting Jack and his family with their kept dark secrets to set them free.

The prettiest flowers grow in the darkest of forest

– CHIEF

Chapter One
Forever Change

Looking down at her bare feet in the passenger's side of the ambulance, Ellie knew her family's life was about to change as they pulled out of the driveway from their farmhouse. She was scared of what the outcome might be. Her husband Jack was in the back with the paramedics working on him while he was fighting for his life. As the ambulance drove the windy back roads of the county heading toward the highway, the EMS driver started asking Ellie questions about Jack, such as his age, health issues, and medications he had been taking. She wasn't sure if his calm questioning was mere fact finding or the reassurance that he was in good hands, because the tears running down her face and silent prayers being said must have been deafening to him over the whirring of the sirens.

The hospital was twenty-five to thirty minutes away, but as Ellie's mind began to wander. She felt she was reliving all the years spent on the farm, having raised their two children and now grandchildren there. Her first thought was remembering finding the property listed online while she was searching for properties for a client and showing it to her husband, as they were looking for more land to raise their kids on so they could ride four-wheelers, hike, hunt, and just be kids. They took a drive past the property, and immediately Ellie was turned off by the muddy brown color the farmhouse was stained, and Jack thought it was a little farther out from town than what he wanted. When they returned to their office they shared in the town of Stenson— she was the broker/owner of Weston Real Estate and Jack was a financial planner—they decided to go ahead and take a serious look at the farm they had just driven by because the ninety acres interested them both.

Ellie scheduled an appointment with the listing agent for the next day, and when they walked through the front door, she instantly fell in love with the possibilities of what it could be, with the hardwood floors, large master bedroom with its own balcony, and with the overall layout of the home. She knew that with its good bones, she could work her magic to turn it into so much more. Jack was immediately drawn to the view out the back door. Once he stepped out onto the deck and looked around at the open field encased by woods, he was sold. Their house on the golf course wasn't on the market yet, but they didn't want to lose out on the farm, as the listing agent mentioned that there were several interested buyers, so Jack and Ellie decided to pull the trigger and buy the property without having their house sold.

The day they closed on the property, they drove out to the farm, and as they got out of their black SUV on that sunny afternoon, they looked around and realized just what a special place they had purchased. The two-story farmhouse sat on a hill overlooking the river bottoms across the road that was planted in Indiana corn. An amazing natural spring flowed out of the hillside behind the two barns, and there was a beautiful blossoming cherry tree in the front yard.

Ellie was snapped back to reality when the ambulance driver told her they were pulling into the back of the ER department at the hospital. Had the drive been that quick? Her thoughts had seemed to take her away for much longer. She quickly threw her shoes on her naked feet and jumped out to follow the gurney in that was carrying Jack. She was instructed to go through another door and that she would be met by a nurse to bring her back to the room. When Ellie walked into the waiting area, she was met by her two children, Chance her twenty-five-year-old son and his wife Mia, and her twenty-four year-old daughter Lauren. She had forgotten they had followed in a vehicle behind the ambulance. They had all been at the farm when the paramedics arrived.

It had been a chaotic scene, as the staircase was too narrow to allow the gurney to travel up them, so all three paramedics grabbed their gear and raced up to the master bedroom to find Jack on the bed in an unresponsive state and breathing erratically. When they realized the seriousness of Jack's condition, they quickly grabbed a blanket and wrapped him up like he was in a hammock and carried him down the stairs. One of the paramedics yelled at Chance to support the underside of the blanket carrying Jack so they could get him safely down the stairs and then to run back up and gather their gear. The paramedics instructed Ellie to grab any medication he had been taking and that they were leaving as soon as Jack was loaded. She had enough time to grab her shoes and cell phone and jump in the passenger's side of the ambulance.

A young, pleasant-faced nurse walked out to the waiting area and told the family they could come back to the room. The halls were extremely quiet because of the 3:00 A.M. hour, and not much talking took place until they entered the ER room where Jack was. It was like a buzzing beehive, with nurses taking instructions from the ER doctor and medical personnel flying in and out of the room. Dr. Minton introduced himself as he kept his attention on Jack while trying to assess his condition. He explained that they were going to intubate him to help with his breathing, as he was still unresponsive, and then he yelled out to a nurse to order a CAT scan for his brain. As the medical team was processing his orders, the doctor turned to the Westons and asked for the chain of events that led them to the ER.

Ellie began to explain that she was sleeping on the couch with her two-and-a-half-year-old granddaughter Alexandra when her daughter Lauren had frantically run down the stairs to say, "Come quick, Dad's breathing isn't good." Ellie jumped up and raced upstairs to their bedroom where Jack was sleeping, and she knew his condition was not good based on his breathing, unresponsiveness, and the fact that his bladder had let go. Ellie quickly jumped into action and moved Jack on his side to help free up his airway and then told Lauren to call 911 and tell them Jack was unresponsive and to send an ambulance immediately.

Lauren's fiancée Leo then entered the bedroom from down the hall where they stayed in a bedroom next to their one-year-old twins Emily and Sophie to see what he could do to help. Lauren asked that he go downstairs to the front door and watch for the paramedics and open it as soon as he could see them pull in. Lauren and her young family had been living with the Westons while their new home was being built next door on the property that Ellie and Jack had purchased a couple of years before. Even though the house could be noisy and busy with three little ones under the age of three running around, she was thankful they were all there at that moment.

Ellie had asked Lauren, "When did you first hear the loud breathing sound?" Lauren explained that she heard her father yell out "Ellie, I need you!" Then Lauren said she heard mumbling and thought her mother had heard Jack and that they were conversing, but then a minute or so later the loud, snoring-like breathing started.

Dr Minton continued with his questions: "Had Jack been ill? And what medications was he currently taking?" Ellie proceeded to answer his questions that Jack was sixty-two years old and had developed a blood clot in his lower left leg and had been taking a blood thinner for the last four days. Jack was concerned about the clot and taking the medication, knowing there were risks to both. Ellie had tried to lightheartedly dismiss his worry, as a lot of people suffered from blood clots with good results in the end, but Jack was still uneasy.

Ellie glanced over at Lauren looking on as they continued to work on her father, and she realized just how difficult this all was for her daughter, since she was so close with Jack. Lauren looked a lot like her father. She was almost five foot five with long legs and had her father's crooked pinkies, but she had her mother's dark-brown hair and freckles. She was beautiful inside and out. Jack had taught Lauren so many things on the farm: how to hit golf balls, shoot a gun, hunt, ride four-wheelers, and drive his truck.

Chance was on the other side of the ER room watching over his father, the only real father he had ever known. Ellie and Jack started dating when

Chance was just three months old. His biological father lived in the same small community but didn't want to be bothered with another child, as he had a young son from a previous marriage. Jack did not have any children and was more than happy to take on the role as his father, and from that point on Jack treated Chance as his own son.

Chance looked a lot like Ellie, with his thin athletic build and sharp facial features; he had turned out to be a very good-looking young man. He was much different than his sister, with his quiet demeanor and moody ways, as he kept most things to himself. Lauren was the complete opposite. She was a social butterfly, she always had a smile on her face, and while growing up she was popular without trying.

A male nurse bustled into the room and announced that he was taking Jack for the CAT scan and would have him right back…Jack was still unresponsive. Chance and Lauren decided to go back to the waiting area where their significant others were anxiously waiting for any new information.

While Ellie sat frozen in a chair in the now empty ER room, in walked Dirk Crumley. He was an undertaker at the local funeral home but had worked for Jack a few years back in the investment world and had remained very good friends. Ellie was surprised to see him. She had just sent out text messages to close friends and family to let them know what was going on with Jack, and Dirk was there thirty minutes later. She definitely needed all the support she could get right then. Dirk had a great sense of humor and was easy on the eye, with his good looks and jet-black hair. Ellie was appreciative that Dirk's wife Tally had told him he needed to get to the hospital and that she and their children would see him later. She was used to him getting calls at all hours, given the line of work he was in.

Ellie was going over everything that had transpired with Dirk when they wheeled Jack back into the room within fifteen minutes after taking him for the scan. Once Jack's bed was placed back to its original position, Ellie went over and kissed his forehead and spoke to him, with no response. Dirk moved to the foot of the bed and began to talk to him as well. Dr. Minton walked back in, followed by Ellie's children, and the bad news started to pour out. He began by saying that he had an opportunity to review the images of the CAT scan and that Jack had suffered one of the worst brain bleeds he had ever seen, and not much more could be done. They all stood there trying to digest what he was saying.

Dr Minton continued on that they would go ahead and move Jack upstairs to the critical care unit and have a neurologist look at him at around at 8:00 A.M...It was already 5:00 A.M. Before the doctor left the ER room, he looked at Ellie and gave his condolences. She realized then that the next few hours were to say goodbye to their family's rock.

The family followed the hospital bed with Jack in it up to the critical care floor, now with Jack's mother May in tow. She had just arrived at the ER with Jack's uncle, as she was old school and didn't drive. The look of such sorrow on her face was hard to bear, knowing she had already buried Jack's brother and father in the last five years, and now soon, Jack.

Once the nurses got Jack situated in the critical care room, Dr. Henson, the attending night physician on the floor, examined his condition and records so he could report his opinion to the family situated in the waiting area. The doctor walked in and took a seat among the red-eyes and wet faces of the family and began the difficult tasks of confirming the medical prognosis of Jack that had already been given downstairs in the ER. He went on to say that the neurologist would make his rounds soon and give his medical opinion as well.

After Dr. Henson left the family to tend to other patients, Ellie went to be with Jack to spend as much time with him as she could. Chance and Lauren followed behind their mother, not only to support her but their father as well. They were a close family and wanted to be there for both their parents.

The hours were ticking by fast for the Westons. Before they realized it, it was 8:00 A.M. and the young neurologist, Dr. Straight, had entered the room to examine Jack. He had already viewed the brain images and now came the final auto-reflex test to determine that Jack was "brain dead." Dr

Straight methodically stepped through all of the various reactor points on the body and gave a thorough explanation as he went about the exam, only to confirm in the end the same conclusion the doctors before him had. Jack was indeed brain dead, and there was nothing more that could be done for him. As he looked into their faces, he knew that if he showed them the brain scans, it would certainly solidify the next step that would need to be taken. Dr. Straight pulled the brain images up on the computer located in Jack's room and went through each image: first was the massive brain bleed, then the image of the left lobe pushing the right lobe into the skull, which caused complete anninhilation of the brainstem. He told the family to take as much time as they needed and that when they were ready the nurses would remove Jack from the ventilator.

Ellie and her children made it back to the waiting area to find it completely full of family and friends. They were amazed and feeling blessed that Jack brought all those people to the hospital at a time when they needed them the most. Ellie filled everyone in on the fact that they were losing Jack and anyone there could go back and say goodbye to him.

Many memories and tears were shared in the waiting area and by Jack's bedside. When Ellie returned to his room, she sat in a chair by Jack holding his hand, laying her head on the bed, sobbing, and telling him things like, she didn't want to say good bye and that she would take their marriage journey all over again with him. It was no secret that both of them were strong-willed and independent-thinking, which could cause marital strife, but it was also understood that they had each other's back in business and family matters and that they had unconditional love for their children and grandchildren. For all the head-butting that came, there was also their great love life, which Jack said was the best part after a heated debate.

The time was not going to be long enough for the family, but heartbroken faces filed in and out of the room for several hours, and some stayed back in the waiting area, as they could not bear to say farewell to the man lying in the hospital bed hooked up to all of the machines keeping him alive.

Jack was not shy about his views on life, family, and business. If he liked someone, they knew it, and if he really liked them, he would do anything for them. He would always say he had a lot of acquaintances but few friends. Jack actually had more friends than he realized.

Twelve long, excruciating hours had passed since they had arrived at the hospital, and one of the critical care nurses came into the room to check on everyone and to see when the family wanted to remove Jack from the ventilator. She emphasized that there was no rush. They needed more questions answered…How long would it take Jack to pass once he was unhooked? Would he be in any pain? The experienced nurse was thorough in her explanations. He would be kept comfortable with medication, and some patients linger for a few days. The nurse felt that given the severity of the brain bleed and damage it did, he would pass quickly.

The Westons knew they were at the final crossroads with Jack and needed to set him free, but they needed some assurance from those closest to them on their timing, as God had already made the decision of Jack's fate. Chance spoke up and suggested he go out to the waiting area and see if Josh Taylor, one of Jack's best friends—even if he was only thirty years old—and Curt Zimmerman, a retired contractor who had worked on projects with Jack, would come back and be with the family for those final moments. Both of them knew Jack well and understood his thoughts on such matters, and both would be a great emotional support for all of them.

The room was full, with Ellie, their children and significant others, and now Josh and Curt. After a conversation among them all, it was unanimous that Jack would not want to lay in that state, and nor would the hospital keep him hooked up more than a couple more days. Chance signaled the nurse to turn off the ventilator, and as Jack's hands were held and tears ran down all their faces, Josh kept his eyes on the heart monitor letting them know that it was slowing down, and finally he saw when the line was flat.

Ellie noticed that Jack looked peaceful and actually had a more youthful look of ten years younger. He had not quite looked himself the last couple of weeks and had spoken of dying to those closest to him and said he was okay with it. The family would later learn that Jack had been having dreams about dying and knew his time was coming. After ten minutes of sobbing, everyone filed out of the room and on into the waiting area to let everyone else know he had passed. Even Jack's mother stayed back, as she could not watch her last son leave this Earth before her.

Slowly the area emptied, and Ellie found herself being escorted to a back parking lot of the hospital by their good friends The Benningtons. They owned a cabin and three hundred acres behind the Weston's farm. Not much was said on the drive back to the farm, which allowed Ellie's thoughts to drift back to the years past. The next memory that came to her was when Chance was thirteen years old and he wanted to repair the barn roof. A panel needed to be tacked back down because the wind had pulled it up, and Jack had told him he could do it after he got home from work, but Chance did not wait. It wasn't thirty minutes from the time Jack dropped the kids off at the farm from picking them up from school that Chance called their office to say he had hurt his arm and thought it was broke. Jack asked what happened, and of course Chance became angry. Knowing his father was right and fearing getting grounded, he hung up his cell phone and waited for his parents to arrive. Ellie rode with Jack, and they found Chance sitting on the ground behind the barn. She asked him to hold up his arm he was holding, and when he did it sank about three inches in the middle. It was obviously broken. The only thing Jack said was, "That is exactly why I told you to stay off the barn roof until I got home…You could have been killed!" Not another word was said as they loaded Chance up to take him to the hospital to have his arm put in a cast.

Jen Bennington spoke up and started to make casual conversation when she peered in the backseat to see Ellie staring out the window looking lost. The conversation trailed off, and Ellie was back to her memories…She had inherited a little money from her grandmother, so she and Jack had decided to put in an in-ground swimming pool for the kids to enjoy there in the country. In fact, the Westons had been known to host special Fourth of July parties out at the farm, and swimming and fireworks were a big hit. Other thoughts of events at the farm quickly ran through her mind, such as the children's birthday parties, prom pictures taken on the covered front porch overlooking the herb garden, and high school graduation celebrations in the back yard. It was hard to believe that their kids were all grown up and having families of their own.

Steve Bennington had been quiet on the drive back. He was always quiet, but he started the conversation next, assuring Ellie that everything was going to be okay and that he and Jen would stay with her the rest of the day. As they pulled up in the drive at the farm, Ellie couldn't believe Jack was gone and what a horrible empty feeling she had in her heart. The Benningtons got Ellie in the door and into the kitchen. That is where everyone always congregated because of its size and the fact that Ellie was always cooking something wonderful. Jen poured her and Ellie a glass of wine and asked Steve to drive into town and pick up some fried chicken at the grocery store. This gave Ellie some time to reflect on all that had happened in the last fifteen hours of her life, and Jen was a good listener. The Weston's lives were forever changed.

After the Benningtons left Ellie that Saturday evening, she went upstairs to the master bedroom and looked around at the large, quiet room. The bed was still in disarray from earlier, so she curled up on it and cried herself to sleep. Ellie was awakened a couple of hours later by the sounds of her two-and-a-half-year-old granddaughter Alexandra (Alexa for short) shrieking through the big farmhouse "Mi Mi . . . Mi Mi." Lauren had arrived back at the farm with her young family in tow and was looking just as lost as Ellie felt.

Ellie had been in communication with her family through the whole ordeal, and her parents had already started their journey up from their winter home in the Florida panhandle, and her twin sister Kelly would be arriving on Sunday. Grant, their younger brother, would be flying in on Monday to help anyway he could.

The next few days were filled with meeting family members at the airport, taking care of pressing business matters for both their busy companies, and going through the arduous tasks of decision-making for Jack's service. Jack didn't much care for weddings or funerals, and he would never let Ellie throw him a birthday party, but she knew this gathering would be huge. Ellie was kept extremely busy, which kept the tears at bay, but when she and her sister went shopping for something to wear to the service, she broke down, and the tears flowed freely. She and Kelly loved to shop, but there was no joy in meandering past the countless racks of clothes and the other happy-go-lucky shoppers. Ellie did not want to say goodbye to Jack. Kelly could see her struggle and told her sister to pick something out she could see herself wearing and they would head back to the farm.

The day came for the service, and all was well orchestrated in every detail, from the most elaborate custom floral arrangement put together by the florist, Patty Clark Jack's childhood friend, to all the family photos of Jack that were synced to the sweetest songs. The funeral posse made up of Jack and Ellie's friends prepared a fantastic potluck dinner and desserts with the precision of a well-trained army, as they had for other funeral services of mutual friends and family. The family arrived at the church's gathering hall to find it busy with final goings-on, with table set up, getting the food out for serving, and tissue boxes being placed on every surface.

Ellie and her children formed the receiving line as people wanting to pay their respects were already lined up at the door. For the next five hours they would receive people of all ages and walks of life, including many young adults that Ellie barely recognized, but recognition came when they were greeted by her children. The farm was a fun safe haven for Lauren and Chance's friends to spend the nights and sometimes several days. The Westons were met by many of Jack's teary-eyed clients. They would tell the family that not only was Jack their financial advisor but their friend, and they felt like they knew each and every one of the them because Jack always talked about his family during his appointments.

Halfway through the evening Ellie sat down at one of the tables with a plate of food and watched the photos projected on a big screen of Jack and their family with all the songs that they carefully chose playing in the back ground...

It was a sweet portrayal of their life . . . of Jack's life. One picture in the lineup caught her eye and triggered her thoughts back to that hot June morning when Jack and Lauren were headed out early so Lauren could play in a tournament. She had just graduated from high school a few weeks before and had played on the high school golf team. Lauren was hoping to play in college but her senior year didn't go quite as planned with her golf game. There were too many distractions, with a new boyfriend and challenging golf tournaments because of headaches and vomiting that were chalked up to nerves.

After graduation she started hitting balls in the next county over at a Big Ten college driving range, and she caught the attention of the driving range attendant. She had also caught the attention of anyone at the range that saw her drives. He asked her if she was on the university team, and Lauren laughed and replied, "No, I would love to be." He then asked her if she knew coach Tinsley. She in fact did know him and had taken lessons from him a couple of years back, so arrangements were made for her to meet and work with him again.

Lauren and the coach got reacquainted, and as he worked with her and saw her improvements and all of the effort she was putting in, he offered her the position of team manager for the women's golf team. He explained that she would be working out and traveling with the team and that if she drastically improved her game, she would hopefully earn a spot. She was excited. In order to have a shot at the opportunity, she needed to improve her game and card some better scores. Lauren and her father, who was also an excellent golfer and was offered a full-ride scholarship to a small university in Florida after he graduated high school, were heading out that morning to a golf tournament a couple of hours away in the southern part of the state. Lauren never made it off the front porch with her golf bag that day. She had gone face-first into the concrete stoop. She had suffered a seizure.

That seemed so long ago, but it had just been six years prior. It took numerous trips to the emergency room at the local hospital and trips to the Cleveland medical clinic to finally get to the diagnosis of epilepsy and then to have the neurologist prescribe the right medication and dosage to keep her seizures under control. It was eighteen years before that monster reared its ugly head, but it was a condition she was born with.

Ellie was brought back to here and now when Jen Bennington found her sitting at the table alone even though the hall was packed. She sat down beside her as she was watching the video of photos. Jen leaned over and whispered to Ellie, "You know, Jack would be pissed with all this fuss," which made Ellie break out in laughter. Jen knew Ellie would find that funny, as they both had a sense of humor. Jen continued, "But you know Jack would have been touched by all the people that came, especially those that traveled from several states away." The evening continued on with condolences and the shock of losing Jack. In fact, a couple of his clients had seen him that very afternoon.

The evening concluded with a small group of family and friends that stayed for a short eulogy with Dirk Crumley officiating and Josh Taylor saying a few final words. Even though Josh liked to cut up and appreciated humor, he had a hard time choking back tears as he spoke, but he was years ahead of his actual age and pulled it off. When the service ended , Ellie and her sister loaded up the keepsakes sent to the family in Jack's memory and headed back to the farm. It was done.

The farmhouse was filled for the next couple of weeks with family members coming and going. Ellie was grateful to have her brother and sister there at the same time because it had been a few years since they were able to all be together; their older sister Bridgett couldn't make it. Even Kelly's daughter Collette had flown in. Ellie hadn't seen her since she was twelve, and Collette was now a sophomore in college out in L. A. Kelly's two older sons had pending engagements they couldn't get out of, and Ellie and her children were sorry they couldn't spend time with them. The cousins always enjoyed hanging out together.

Ellie's parents and Jack's mother lived within five miles of the farm, so they were all able to share a few meals, tears, and laughter while everyone was in town. Jack had a way of doing that—being "peacemaker" and bringing everyone together. They all loved each other, but they all didn't always see eye to eye on family matters, and there would be Jack encouraging someone to pick up the phone and break the silence. He would always say, "Someone could die tomorrow, and you would be sorry you didn't set your differences aside… It is what it is."

Chapter Two
Adjustments

Ellie was pushed back into the daily grind of everyday life, without Jack. She had several real estate transactions that were already in the works when her life was turned upside down that needed her attention, as well as her grandchildren and pets. After long days, Ellie would go home in the evenings to a house that seemed too still, even though there were others there. She couldn't quite put her finger on it. Was all the white noise in her head grief? Why hadn't she had any dreams about Jack when others had? Ellie had been keeping Jack's cell phone charged. She was hoping for a sign…a message from Jack, but up until then, nothing.

On day twenty after Jack's passing, Lauren had called her mother after dropping off the girls at the sitters as she was headed to the office. She was crying. "What's wrong, Lauren?" Ellie asked.

Lauren began, "I was at the farm getting the girls ready to leave when I felt someone watching me. I turned around and it was dad! He found a way to make contact with me." Ellie wasn't sure what to think, so she told Lauren to drive safe and that she would see her at the office shortly and she could give her mother all the details when she got there.

Ellie wasn't surprised with Lauren's encounter with Jack, as she herself always had a sixth sense, had seen apparitions, had dreams that were premonitions, and understood there was "life" beyond this one, whatever form it was.

Both Jack and Ellie believed in God and were spiritual people without attending church much. Jack's father was a Baptist minister, and he grew up spending a lot of time in church, whether he wanted to or not.

Lauren came into Ellie's office once she arrived and proceeded to describe what had happened. She said she felt extremely heavy before seeing his presence, and when she initially saw him, he was very faded looking. Jack told his daughter, "Mimic these exact hand movements," as he demonstrated what to do, and after she completed the same motions, he came into clear focus. Lauren said he was wearing one of his plaid shirts, a vest, and blue jeans," which was his usual farm attire. "I just stood there frozen and listened to all that he said." Jack told her to remember the numbers 8426. He showed Lauren a hand-drawn picture and said her mother would know what that meant, and lastly he told Lauren, "Whenever you want to reach out to me, complete the special hand motions I showed you, and I will appear. Make sure your mother is with you so I can speak with you both". After Jack spoke, his image started to fade and it closed up into a sphere. He was no longer visible.

Lauren was extremely shaken by the event and told her mother she did not want to be at the farm by herself. It was quiet for two or three days until one night when Ellie had fallen asleep on the couch with Alexa while they were watching a movie, and something woke her. When Ellie opened her eyes, the TV screen was grainy looking, and there was Jack! She was so terrified, she closed her eyes and opened them a couple of minutes later, and he was still there. Now he was sitting in an overstuffed armchair peering out from the TV at her and not speaking. That was more terrifying. Ellie closed her eyes again for a minute or so, and when she reopened them, the screen had horizontal lines going back and forth on it, and suddenly the TV screen flipped back to the movie they had been watching. Was that a dream? She had never heard of such events happening. She didn't know why she was so frightened by it because she knew Jack wasn't there to cause harm but to communicate to.

Ellie woke Lauren early the next morning and explained to her what had happened with the TV and asked her if she could do the special hand movements to make her father come forward. She needed to know if that was indeed Jack himself; both her and Lauren had many questions for him. They both headed for the stairs without another word and headed into the formal dining room and took a seat at the long dining table. Ellie watched Lauren go through the hand movements… She drew three imaginary lines across the palm of each hand, held her palms up and out away from her body, and then she turned them down and flipped them back up. After Lauren completed the movements, she closed her eyes as she held her hands out for a minute or so, and when she opened them, she said "He's here."

Ellie asked where, and Lauren pointed to the other side of the table. "He is standing there by the primitive table with the lamp on it."

She could not see what her daughter could see but had no doubt he was there. Ellie began the conversation. "Was that you in the TV last night Jack?"

"Yes, I had been trying to reach out to you, Ellie, but you are hard-headed and that was the only way so far."

Ellie smiled at his hard-headed comment. "I didn't mean to ignore you. I was just startled." Jack continued on. He showed Lauren the same piece of paper with a piece of wood on it, and she asked, "What does that mean?"

Jack replied, "Ellie, you know Mr. Woods likes you and has interest in pursuing you." Ellie was surprised by his comment, as Mr. Woods was a textile representative Ellie had done business with a few years back and Jack had suspicioned that there was more to it.

"Jack, I am not interested in Mr. Woods, and it saddens me that we have so much more to talk about other than things from the past that have no merit."

Lauren chuckled and said, "Mom, Dad is telling you to calm down, and he is taking his hands and pumping them up and down in gesture." Ellie was teary-eyed but still managed to snicker a little at the conversation.

Lauren then asked her father, "Did I see you sitting in the red Chevy truck in the barn when I went to feed the dogs yesterday evening?"

Jack replied, "Yes, I was keeping watch because I saw a strange man I didn't recognize rummaging around the barn, and I got cold." Lauren and Ellie were more curious about the fact that he felt cold than there being a strange man in the barn. Jack continued on. "I still have some sensation to temperatures." The days and nights were getting cooler, as it was now the start of November.

Jack said he was okay and happy but that he needed to go now, as he was limited on time. "I love and miss you and I will be back soon." His image faded and closed into a sphere as it had the previous visit, and he was gone. Ellie was hoping Jack would be able to come directly to her and communicate, but if this was the only way, she would just have to accept it and feel blessed that they were able to communicate at all.

Lauren sat a little longer at the table. She told Ellie that when her father comes, it drains her. Ellie wasn't sure if the reason she felt that way was because of the event itself or because of the epilepsy. Maybe that's how Jack was able to reach out to Lauren was because of her medical condition and the fact that she took medication to slow down her brain to avoid seizures. Ellie was thankful she could lean on her daughter right now. It was usually the other way around. When Lauren started having seizures and seeking medical treatment, she relied on her parents a lot because she was unable to drive a car for over a year. Ellie knew what a lost sense of freedom that had to have been for Lauren.

Leo and Lauren had broken up during that time period, shortly after she was diagnosed. Jack and Ellie thought it was because he didn't want to be saddled with someone that had a medical condition and wanted the freedom that most twenty-one-year-old's have. The break-up was short-lived, and much to the Weston's dismay, they were back together again. It was no secret that her parents were not fond of him in the beginning. They felt he was too immature and liked to spend all of his money, and hers, on things that interested him. But as time went on and they began a family of their own, her parents could see that Lauren's kind ways and her family's hard work ethic were starting to have an effect on Leo.

When Lauren carried their first child, it was pretty uneventful, but immediately after the birth of Alexandria came another wave of medical problems. About a month after the delivery, Lauren's gall bladder went bad, and she had to have it removed. Ellie remembered being in the recovery room when they wheeled Lauren out of surgery, and things were just off. Lauren was behaving oddly, saying weird things that just weren't her. Ellie and Leo questioned the nurses but were assured that her behavior was normal after going under anesthetics. Three days later, Lauren was rushed to the hospital in horrible pain only to be told that the pain was normal, her blood work was fine, and to go home and rest. It took two more trips to the ER after that and Lauren being in critical shape before they gave a serious look and realized she had a bile duct leak and needed to be rushed back into surgery. Lauren's blood pressure was 200 over120. Dr. Prather was in charge of the surgery triage, and he told Lauren while they were prepping her for the emergency surgery that recovery would be long and that she would be in a lot of pain for quite a while.

It took her three months and three additional procedures to get her back upright. Lauren had lost all that time with her newborn that she couldn't get back. The first surgery had gone so wrong, and they would later discover that the surgeon had cut the bile duct and lacerated her abdominal cavity, she had lost two pints of blood and had suffered a seizure on the operating table. It was a miracle that she came out of the whole ordeal okay.

After Jack's visit, they got up from the table, and Ellie told Lauren she would go ahead and get the girls up so they could get to the office. Leo had already left for his construction job a couple of hours before. When Ellie pulled up in front of the office building that she had shared with Jack, she just sat there not wanting to start another day without him. She glanced over to the car parked next to her and caught sight of one of her clients and realized she didn't have a choice but to jump out of her SUV with a smile on her face and walk to the front door.

A couple more days passed when Lauren came to her mother around 11:00 P.M. and said, "Dad's here." Ellie followed her daughter back into the formal living/dining where they had conversed with Jack previously and took a seat at the table. Jack immediately started to speak. "I forgot to mention during the last visit, Ellie, that when your brother and sister were here at the farmhouse sitting around the kitchen island and you all were talking and laughing, I was here and so was your father, and he was glad to see all of you together and getting along." Ellie's father Lance had passed seven years prior, and she was surprised to hear that he was there…She was certain he immediately went to a darker place. She loved her father, but her stepfather was the one that raised them all, took care of them, and loved them. Lance wasn't really in Ellie's life after the age of eight when her parents divorced. He was college educated and always held executive positions in major corporations, but he was an alcoholic who spent more time in bars, chasing women, and gambling than he did at home. That's why her mother divorced him. Ellie's father started coming around after she started having her own children, and his health started to fail because of his past. She would be respectful toward him but really didn't like him as a person.

Jack went on to say that he was starting to develop emotions now, such as anger and sadness. He said he would understand if Ellie decided to move on to another relationship in the future but that he would be sad about it. Ellie held up her left hand in the air. "I think I am pretty committed and have no desire to change my life." When Ellie's sister Kelly was home for those two weeks after Jack passed, they decided to get a tattoo at the age of fifty-two. Kelly put her children's names on the inside of her wrist, and Ellie had Jack's initials put on her ring finger…She wasn't going anywhere.

Lauren continued to relay Jack's message: "I am very proud of both of you for taking care of business and things that need to be done around the farm. I have to go now. I only have so much time per visit and only so much time for the year, then I have to move on, but I am trying to stay longer." Jack was good at negotiating deals and Ellie and Lauren were hoping he would put his biggest deal together for them to have more time, no matter the existence. "I love you all and give my best friend a hug and kiss for me." He was talking about Alexa. He had formed a strong bond with her, and Jack took her everywhere with him when he wasn't at work.

Lauren looked at her mother and said, "That was different!"

"What do you mean?" Ellie looked puzzled.

"Dad just flew right by me. he must be getting his sea legs," Lauren said. Both Lauren and Ellie laughed at that, even though their cheeks were damp. They missed Jack terribly.

The family went on with the handling of everyday tasks of unfinished business at the farm and office. Chance was good to stop by for support since Jack's passing, sometimes accompanied by Mia, and would do little things to help his mother that might have gone undone for a while. After Jack started making his appearances, Ellie pulled Chance aside and told him what had been going on and said, "Please keep an open mind if your father reaches out to you and don't be afraid." Chance didn't always have the same beliefs his mother did, and she could tell by his lack of curiosity he didn't quite believe what Ellie and Lauren had been experiencing. He agreed half-heartedly, but Ellie was hopeful Chance would have the opportunity to experience what they had. It was a gift.

The month of November seemed to fly by on into the Thanksgiving holiday. Just the immediate family showed and enjoyed the somber meal, and they made it through. After everyone left, Ellie got the kitchen cleaned up from the big feast and then wandered upstairs to Jack's walk-in closet and sat on the floor smelling in the faint scent of his cologne and just staring up at his crisply ironed dress shirts, still in disbelief that he was gone. Several minutes had passed, and she decided to get herself busy again. She started cleaning her walk-in closet when she came across the bag with the cutest woodland fairy Halloween costumes in it. She began to sob. Ellie had purchased them for all three of Lauren's children. They didn't make it out to the Halloween festivities, and the costumes still had their tags on them because Jack had passed four days prior. Ellie thought they might get another visit from Jack that day or the next since it was the first Thanksgiving holiday without him, and when morning came, so did Jack. Ellie was bustling around the kitchen and the girls were playing in the family room where she could keep an eye on them, when Lauren rounded the corner to say, "He's here." Ellie immediately stopped her work and went into the formal dining room with Lauren. It was quiet in there with no distractions of a TV or little ones. Jack began this visit by telling Lauren not to use the hand signals anymore because he had trouble getting through because of other spirit intervention, as they were taking it as an open invitation. Lauren quickly agreed. Next on Jack's mind was reprimanding Ellie. "When you go on a walk in the creek bed and woods, you need to take your gun," even though she always walked with their large red-haired German shepherd Red and felt safe. Ellie enjoyed her long walks because it gave her a chance to be alone with her thoughts, and she enjoyed looking for artifacts, fossils, and semi-precious stones. Their farm was once an ancient lake, and it was nothing but sand underneath the green grass, and interesting finds were left behind from the ice sheets that traveled from much farther north during the ice age. "I can't always be with you on those two-plus-hour walks, and there is only so much I can do to protect you." Ellie wasn't sure why Jack was so bothered by her last walk…Maybe he had seen the bobcat they had viewed on their hunting camera during last hunting season that was the size of Red. Had it been following them? Whatever the worry, Ellie agreed to carry her gun.

Jack went on to the next subject. "I have met another spirit here on the farm. He said his name was Mathews. He says he suffered a horrible death and that he is buried here on the farm. He also spoke about his parents being extremely wealthy and that they were here before houses were built in the area. They owned our farm and everything a mile south and half-mile deep. Ellie quickly thought about the age of the oldest part of the farmhouse, and she remembered that it dated back to the mid 1800s. Jack went on to say that Mathews said he was thirty-two years old when he died, but Jack thought he looked twenty years older. He also mentioned he had sandy-colored hair and looked like he was wearing some kind of uniform." He is quiet and polite. He says that he stayed here because he loves it."

Ellie was intrigued to hear about the spirit on their farm and was very interested to learn more. "Can you find out more information about him and his people, Jack?"

"Yes Ellie. I will see if he will tell me more next time I see him. He hangs out at the Sugar Shack a lot because he says it is peaceful there." Ellie thought, *wow, that's not too far from the house.* It was an old, three-sided building that the Westons pushed over with a tractor a few years back that had been used years ago by previous owners as a structure to make maple syrup in. The Westons were told when they bought the property that many years ago the farm was much larger and that it was a working orchard. People would travel for miles in horse and buggy to get fruit for their cellars and fill their barrels with water from the spring.

Ellie's thoughts went to the pool because that was only two hundred feet or so from the shack and a clear view from it. When their children were growing up and they weren't home for the day during the swimming season, she and Jack would skinny dip, lounge on floats, and sip on whatever tasty adult beverage Jack had whipped up for their "hang out sessions" on those lazy Sundays. Not to mention the steamy nights in the hot tub that sat directly behind the pool. Ellie just smiled and thought poor Mathews had to be traumatized by the Weston's free-spirited ways, but she hoped he had given them privacy.

Lauren said, "He has to go now. He loves us, and he will see us soon." When Jack left the visits now, Ellie noticed that Lauren would look down at her cell phone. It was always in her hand, like every young person these days. Ellie asked, "Why do you look down at your phone after you say he has to go?"

Lauren replied, "Because it makes me sad to see him leave."

The brief silence was broken by one of the twins crying in the next room. Most likely Alexandria ripped a toy out of one of the twin's hands as she shouted "Mine!" at her. Alexa was at that age now, and the twins were now fourteen months old and into everything, including Alexa's stuff.

The days started to turn into weeks as the family was learning to adjust to the loss of Jack and weaving in and out of constant new adjustments that life brought them. The month of December quickly came, and by week two, Jack had made another appearance. The twins and Leo were fast asleep upstairs, and Lauren came down to the family room, where Ellie was just dozing off on the couch with Alexa and nudged her mother and said, "Come on. . . ." Ellie knew he was there. She looked at her cell phone. It was 11:30 P.M. She climbed off the couch slowly so she wouldn't wake her sleeping grandchild.

They tiptoed into the dining room and took a seat. Jack said he didn't have much time and asked them if they had any questions. Ellie always asked, "How are you?"

Jack started his reply, "I am starting to sleep a little now."

Lauren and Ellie glanced at each other, and Ellie spoke up. "I didn't think spirits grew tired...Where do you sleep?

Jack answered her question. "Yes, spirits get tired, especially when they visit loved ones. It drains their energy force." Jack continued "I sleep here in the farmhouse sometimes and sometimes in heaven...It's a peaceful sleep." He continued on with more interesting information. "I have also been eating a little food. I am not hungry, but I enjoy the slight taste I can experience, and before you ask . . . no, I do not go to the bathroom." Lauren giggled at her father, knowing he would have asked such a question himself. "Ellie, I know you have been leaving the TV upstairs in our bedroom on for me, and I appreciate that because I can't turn it on, but I can flip through the channels once it's on.

Jack continued through Lauren. "I would love to see a fresh-cut Christmas tree here in the formal dining room. I love the pine scent, and you can set the white artificial tree up in the family room." Ellie said she would try and get one bought this year, but she was amused by his request. In the past when she would take the time to pick out that perfect fresh-cut tree and bring it home, Jack would moan and groan that he had to help put it up and take it down. The taking down was the real chore because dried needles would go everywhere and there would be Jack shoving the tree through the front door, making an even bigger mess as he drug it down to the burn pile while mumbling under his breath that Ellie just needed to put up the artificial tree and keep it simple. Ellie grinned and said, "I think that's a great idea, Jack, and I hope I have time to pick one up this year".

Ellie would normally have had the Christmas decorations up before now, including having the four columns on the front porch wrapped in hundreds of twinkling lights, but she was having a hard time feeling the holiday joy. Lauren spoke up and said, "He has to go. He loves us both and will see us soon." He was gone.

Things had slowed down a little at the office due to the holidays, and Ellie was thankful she could take some time to spend with family and friends. She enjoyed a couple of dinners out with Chance and Mia, as well as a dinner in at the farm with the Benningtons. Ellie hadn't seen the Benningtons since Jack's service, and she was looking forward to her and Jen enjoying a bottle of wine and cackling at all the oddities of life. Poor Steve was always the designated driver so that the girls could let their hair down and let a little "steam out of the pot," as he would say, but he actually didn't mind because they were all able to enjoy the conversations no matter where it took them, whether it be politics, death, gardening, family. Steve was very laid back, even though he came from wealth and all that comes with it, and Jen was a little earthy, which created that perfect balance for him. She was an accomplished glass blower and talented at everything she put her hands into, from anything art-related, to designing her dream kitchen, to gardening and cooking.

Jen walked in the side entryway leading to the kitchen and yelled out her usual, "How's it going?" This always made Ellie smile not so much the question as Jen always had a smile on her face when she asked. They never came empty-handed. In one hand Jen was carrying some crafted beer and in the other pork carnitas, and Steve was following close behind her, juggling a huge chocolate sheet cake.

As the beer tops flew off and Ellie whipped up some chips and dipping sauce she had been perfecting for such occasions, the evening began. Once they had a couple of beers thrown back, Ellie began to tell them about all that had been happening around the farm and with Jack. Jen and Steve were intrigued with all that they were told and had no doubt about Ellies truths. Jen, like Ellie, wanted to know more about the spirit named Mathews. Most likely his parents also owned their property as well at the time. Jen said, "Let us know what else you find out. This is really fascinating." Jen was very opened-minded to such things in this world and beyond. After a couple of hours of laughing, solving the world's problems, and even shedding a few tears, the Benningtons needed to get home to let their dogs out, so they said their goodbyes and promised to get together soon. Ellie loved spending time with them.

The Spring

Chapter Three
Sweet Babies

By the third week in December, Ellie had the Christmas decorations up, but she ran out of time to get a fresh tree bought at her favorite nursery, which was an hour away from the farm. She also didn't get the front-porch columns wrapped in lights, but she did hang a pretty wreath on the front door...She still wasn't in the Christmas spirit.

One evening while the girls were in their highchairs eating dinner and watching cartoons . . . Jack came.

Lauren was sitting at the kitchen island while Ellie was finishing up dinner preparations. "Dad's here . . . and he said to just stay put, we can talk here in the kitchen." Ellie stopped whipping the pan of mashed potatoes so she could give her full attention to the conversation.

Jack began, "I have brought Grayson Mae with me a few times to visit her sisters." This was exciting and surprising news to both Ellie and Lauren. Jack continued, "She looks exactly like Emily and Sophie, and she is the same size as the twins. Babies continue to grow in heaven." Maybe that's why Lauren and Leo could hear the twins laughing and shrieking through the bedroom walls sometimes after they put them to bed in the evening. Jack said she was just as feisty as the other two.

Ellie was so struck by the wonderment of what Jack was telling them because Grayson Mae was Emily's identical twin, and she was an acardiac twin.

She was born without a heart, and it was Emily that kept her alive and growing. The baby was also born without a leg, arm, face, and other organs

Jack also mentioned he had seen his father a couple of times and his good friend Trent Bearman who had passed away three years prior. "I haven't seen my brother yet." Ellie didn't ask why, as they were as different as night and day and didn't have much in common. The only time he really saw his brother while he was living was at family gatherings. "I haven't seen Mathews lately, but I'm sure I will soon. It's time for me to go…I love you all and wish I could be there." Lauren and Ellie knew that he meant he wished he could be there physically with them all, but he was always there.

He was gone…

Leo was working late, so Ellie helped Lauren with the girls that evening, and once they were all tucked in bed, she sat down with a glass of wine in hand and reflected on what Jack said at his visit that evening. Her thoughts drifted back to when Lauren first found out she was expecting twins. She was surprised, but she shouldn't have been, since twins ran in their family. Lauren would always joke with her brother that it would be him that would have twins, but so far Chance and Mia didn't have any children, but his mother was hoping they would eventually.

Ellie drove Lauren to every OB/GYN appointment because as her pregnancy progressed, her hormone levels changed, and her body chewed through her seizure meds faster, making her more susceptible to having seizures. Ellie would always go back to the exam room with Lauren so she could watch the progress of the pregnancy. Lauren was about two months along when Ellie noticed on the ultrasound screen that there was more than two sacs, and she asked the doctor, "Is that a third sac?"

He reluctantly said, "Yes, it is what we call a disappearing twin. It has abnormalities and is not growing correctly. They usually terminate themselves and the body absorbs it. We thought that would have happened already." Lauren was shocked to find out there were three…

In the first three months of gestation she had to have an appointment with a genetics counselor because of the genetic defect that took place. It was explained to her that when the fertilized egg had split, not all of the DNA was captured by the division when the second embryo was formed. The baby would never make it to full-term. But they were wrong. She was the "white unicorn" and would surpass all odds. Ellie had asked a few OB/GYN physicians that had practiced for at least thirty years if they had ever seen an acardiac twin born, and the response was always the same…No, they never make it to birth.

The OB/GYN practice had her coming in every two weeks to monitor the babies and for her to see the neonatal specialist. They would do an ultrasound at every visit to see if the third baby was still growing, and much to the doctor's disbelief, all three babies kept growing week after week, and by the fourth month the doctors were prepping Lauren that she most likely would lose all of them, because at that point if the third one died, it could cause her to go into labor and cause a chain reaction that they couldn't stop.

The other concern was that the acardiac identical twin's heart was pumping the blood for both of them, since the acardiac baby was missing a heart. The identical twin was the "pump" twin. Their umbilical cords were tethered close together in the placenta, and that is how the baby was able to pump the blood for both.

The neonatal specialist referred Lauren to a children's research hospital out of state that could perform a special procedure to crimp the cord of the acardiac twin to stop the blood flow if the ultrasound revealed she was causing her twin's heart to become enlarged and eventually cause heart failure. Lauren and Leo went together on the first two trips and met with Dr Raj Hinchman. He was head of neonatal research there, and he was extremely good-looking, soft-spoken, and charismatic. The first trip went as they expected, but by the second trip, Dr. Hinchman was trying to talk them into delivering the babies there so that they could keep the acardiac twin for research and do testing/monitoring on her identical twin for a couple of weeks. Leo and

Lauren said definitely not, that it was too far from home and that they did not want their baby to be put in a specimen jar and dissected.

Ellie went with Lauren on the third trip to the children's research hospital because Leo couldn't go, and they stayed at the hotel next to the hospital. Lauren's appointments started early the next day, and when she was done they were heading back home. It was a several hour drive from the farm. They finally finished up the day with Dr Hinchman, and he stuck to the testing outcome and didn't mention the babies being delivered there, most likely because Ellie was there and he probably sensed she would be a little more direct with him.

Lauren then spoke up and informed him that it was too far for her to drive for his team to monitor the babies when they were doing the same at the OB/GYN and with the neonatal specialist back home. If they felt the twins were in danger and she needed that procedure done, she would be back. There were only five hospitals in the US that had the capability to perform that particular procedure.

Dr Hinchman didn't say much at the visit, but a few days later he called Lauren on her cell phone and said she wasn't thinking about the welfare of her babies and that they wanted the acardiac twin for research. "That is not a baby, and it has no soul" were his words to manipulate her into handing over the doomed twin.

Lauren's response was "Fuck you!" and she hung up the phone. She couldn't believe that she said that to a doctor, but she also couldn't believe he was trying to coerce her into handing over her child. No matter the deformities, she was beautiful in her eyes and in God's.

The months kept rolling on, and the babies kept growing and thriving in the womb. The doctors were amazed. Dr Lisdon was going to be the delivery doctor, and every time she walked through the examining room door and saw Lauren sitting there on the exam table she would smile really big and say, "I can't believe you made it to another appointment." All the doctors there were amazed the babies were holding on. "Whatever you are doing, keep it up because it's working." As Dr. Lisdon exited the room Lauren told her she would keep praying.

Up to thirty-two weeks, Lauren had been doing well with the pregnancy. Then one day she started to have horrible pains that felt like contractions that caused her to have seizures that would leave her unconscious for several minutes. After the third episode in three days left her unconscious for thirty minutes, Leo loaded her up and took her to the emergency room. When they did a blood draw, the physician realized her seizure medication levels were too low, and they felt that was causing her problem, so they upped her dosage on her prescriptions and pumped her full of extra medication. Someone miscalculated. By the time Leo got her back to the farm, she was vomiting profusely, and that lasted all night. Ellie suspicioned that Lauren was suffering from a drug overdose.

When dawn came, Leo loaded her back in the car and rushed her to the ER, and she was immediately admitted into the critical-care unit. Her potassium and blood pressure were fatally low. God was still answering her prayers. She was still having contraction-like pains, but they weren't contractions. The OB/GYN doctor overseeing her there deducted that the acardiac twin most likely had cysts on her that were rupturing and letting bacteria into the sac, so they put her on a high-powered antibiotic, and within twenty-four hours the pains had stopped.

It was week thirty-four of the pregnancy, and Lauren started having real contractions one afternoon, so Ellie took her into the OB/GYN office, and when Dr Lisdon examined her, she found that she was in fact having hard labor pains. Lauren was instructed to go to the delivery floor at the hospital and that they would have a bed ready for her. They were going to give Lauren a medication to try to stop the contractions, as well as a high dosage of steroids to help with the babies' lungs. They were six-and-a-half weeks from their due date and pretty small. By the time Lauren checked in and was being wheeled up to her room, Leo was there waiting for her at the elevator doors when they opened.

Within a couple of hours the medication had started to work, and when Dr Lisdon stopped in to check the progress, she said she would be releasing them the next morning. Ellie headed on back to the farm to help Jack with Alexa and fill him in on everything. It was around six that morning when Ellie got the call while walking their dogs. Lauren was in full-blown labor and heading into delivery. She hurried and jumped in the shower before she left because she knew they would have to prep Lauren for a c-section and that it would take a little bit.

By the time Ellie arrived at the delivery waiting area, Lauren had already been rushed into delivery, so all Ellie could do was sit there and wait. She took a seat and started thinking back to the discussions she and Lauren had about the third baby she was going to have to say goodbye to as soon as she was delivered, and Lauren still wasn't prepared for that even though she had several months to come to terms with it.

The birth plan was well spelled out for the OB/GYN practice. The acardiac twin was to be wrapped in a blanket and placed in Lauren's arms while she passed. Ellie feared that the delivery doctor was being pressured by Dr. Hinchman to collect the acardiac twin and send her on to the research hospital, so she drafted a document for her attorney to execute for Lauren and Leo with their wishes for their baby after she was born. They would agree to photos of all three babies, being able to keep a blood sample and the placenta with the umbilical cords attached for future research, and nothing more. Lauren had already made prior arrangements for Dirk Crumley to pick up the baby after they had spent as much time as they needed with her and said their initial goodbyes. Ellie was not surprised when the doctor refused to sign the document. She said she couldn't sign on behalf of the hospital. Ellie's suspicions were spot on.

It was about two hours after Ellie arrived at the hospital when Leo came out, still in his scrubs, and said she could come back. Lauren was back in her room. While they walked that direction, Leo filled her in that Emily and Sophie weighed 3.6 and 3.4 pounds respectively and were doing as well as could be expected for preemies. They were being taken care of in the NICU unit, and they probably wouldn't be able to see them for a few more hours.

When Ellie entered the room, she thought Lauren looked wrung out and kind of sad…Ellie knew why. Lauren went on to tell her about the delivery and then pointed to a tiny hand-woven cloth basket sitting next to her on the bed and asked, "Do you want to see Grayson Mae?" Ellie said, "Of course I want to hold her." She walked over and picked up the basket and lifted out the small bundle that was wrapped in a newborn baby knit cap. Ellie reached inside and pulled out the sweetest baby's head…Grayson Mae had the same dark hair as her sisters'. Her head was softer to the touch than the others. She had one ear and no face.

Ellie immediately asked, "Where's the rest of her?"

Lauren spoke up and said the delivery doctor had told them that her body was falling apart and that was the best they could do. Ellie knew exactly what happened…They took the rest of her for research.

Ellie asked then, "Why didn't you tell the doctor to clip her together and wrap her in a blanket?" She was just so bothered by the doctor's lack of respect for what Lauren wanted for her child.

Leo piped up and said, "It was a crazy scene. They rushed us into delivery, and Lauren was very upset because she knew the babies were coming too soon, and I was trying to keep her calm so she wouldn't have a seizure. When they delivered the babies, they weren't breathing at first. It was all going so fast, and our attention was on the twins that could be saved." Ellie decided her questions would be best saved for the doctor at a later time. The family was so excited to have the babies here, and Ellie and Jack were looking forward to watching them grow up on the farm, even though they would be sleeping next door when their house was finished.

• • •

Ellie was jarred awake, to the here and now, when their little dog Zeek jumped up onto her lap. She had drifted off to sleep and still had the glass of wine in her hand when she came to. Ellie turned off the TV and dragged herself upstairs to crawl into her comfy bed with Zeek following close behind. He was a mountain feist and had the best disposition. Zeek knew no strangers, whether they were on two or four legs, and was loving to all. Zeek liked to burrow under the covers, which used to bother Ellie because of the dog hair, but she was more accepting now since the other side of the bed was empty.

The Christmas holiday came and went without too many obligatory dinners and appearances. Ellie still had Jack's side of the family in for a casual dinner. Some traveled up to two hundred miles to attend on Christmas Eve, and Christmas Day was reserved for Ellie, her children and grandchildren at the farm. Ellie had surprised Lauren and Chance with twenty-five thousand-dollar checks to each of them, and in the memo lines on the checks she wrote "Love Dad." Jack had mentioned to Ellie a couple of months before he passed that he wanted to put their kids on the smaller life insurance policy as beneficiaries. Ellie was fine with that, but he never got around to it…His time came too soon, so Ellie honored what was meant to be.

The three girls had a fun time opening their gifts, with only one fight amongst them. Sophie and Alexa got into a tug of war with the new blanket that Alexa opened, which was quite entertaining. After all the mess was cleaned up, Chance and Lauren had to go to Christmas at their significant others' family gatherings. Both of them felt bad for leaving Ellie, but she was looking forward to a little peace and quiet and maybe even a nap.

The following week at the office, Ellie and Lauren were in Ellie's office on the second floor going over the day's to-do list, and Lauren suddenly quit speaking and Ellie thought she heard footsteps. "Did you hear that, Lauren? I thought I heard footsteps on the stairs."

Lauren glanced at the doorway and broke out in a grin and said, "Someone came to work with us today." That made Ellie smile. "Good Morning Jack."

Jack leaned up against the copy machine and quickly got the conversation going. "I have seen my brother, and he is with his first wife. They were expecting a child when she passed away from brain cancer." Ellie wasn't sure if Jack's mother even knew that. Sally had passed before Ellie and Jack had met, and by then his brother Edward was already married to his second wife. They had met at the hospital on the oncology floor; she was one of Sally's nurses. Jack continued. "She is still pregnant, and she feels flutters in her from the baby kicking. She will always remain pregnant. Her and Edward are happy they are together again."

Ellie was glad to know that Jack was spending time with his brother. He also mentioned he had seen his father a couple more times but that when his father starts asking him what has he missed the last few years, it makes Jack sad that he is not with Ellie and his family, so he stays close to them in the farmhouse and doesn't visit with others in heaven too much. He doesn't want to miss a thing.

Jack went on to say that the first edition of the book *The Bread and Butter Indian* was worth quite a bit of money. Ellie made a mental note to look in the children's playroom upstairs in the farm house. There was a bookcase filled with children's books from when Lauren and Chance were growing up, as well as some older books from Ellie's childhood. She thought she remembered seeing that book on one of the shelves, but it had been a while.

It was time for Jack to go. "I love you and will see you soon." He was gone. The office phone started to ring, throwing Ellie and Lauren back into the workday.

After the start of the new year, the winter season finally brought a decent amount of snow that was heavy and wet, which made for good sledding, so Leo bundled Alexa up, and out the door they went to find the long sled in one of the barns. Lauren called out to Ellie, "You have to come see this!" Leo and Alexa were sledding down the big hill on the side of the house and Hauser, their big rottweiler, would run alongside them and yank Alexa's hat off as they were going down the hill. It was pretty cold out, so the sledding didn't last long, and the last few minutes were spent throwing snowballs to their energetic dog; he was actually pretty good at catching them.

Chance called later that day to say he would be out to push snow off the drive and then he was meeting Steve Bennington there because they were going back to the Bennington's property to target practice. Ellie was hoping Jen would tag along so she could visit with her. She was good medicine for Ellie.

The following Sunday Ellie received a call from her mother-in-law May. She had gone out to shovel snow off her sidewalk that has an incline up to the detached garage, and she had fallen. May was eighty-seven years old and very independent. she liked to do such tasks herself and not bother anyone. Ellie knew once May said she had fallen and heard a loud pop that she needed to go to the hospital. She had broken her shoulder. Ellie was amazed she was able to pick herself up off the ground and get herself back inside after suffering such an injury.

After Ellie gingerly placed May in her vehicle and headed toward the hospital, May piped up. "I am so mad at myself for falling. I knew better than to go out and do that." Chance had already told his grandmother he would be over later that day to shovel snow for her. "I don't know about you, but I dread walking into that place." May was talking about the hospital. It had only been two and a half months earlier that they were forced to say good bye to Jack there.

Once May's left arm was put in a sling to stabilize her shoulder, they headed back towards Jack's childhood home. "You know, Ellie. It was hard losing Edward Sr. and Edward, but losing Jack has been unbearable." Ellie knew just what she meant. Jack was May's go-to guy when she needed something, whether it was a question about medical insurance or something needing fixed, he would know who to call. Jack was much more than that. He was also her confidant, especially when it came to their family's inner-workings. He was good at giving her great sensible advice.

When Jack's father passed, it was up to him to get his mother where she needed to be. The most frequented trip was to the super store in the next town over for groceries every Sunday. After Alexa came along and then hit the one-month-old mark, she would also make the journey to buy groceries. Jack would put her baby carrier on a flatbed cart and place groceries all around her and talk to her as they strolled the aisles. Ellie remembered that on one of the shopping outings when Jack was talking to Alexa, as he was passing by a young man handing out food samples and Jack asked, "Are you mean mugging me?" The store employee didn't see the baby tucked in between all the groceries, and he answered Jack, "No sir!" Jack just laughed and pointed down at Alexa and said, "I was talking to her, sorry." They all laughed.

Jack, May, and Alexa were all expected at the super store on Sundays for the weekly pilgrimage for groceries. All the employees enjoyed watching Alexa grow from her baby carrier to the busy toddler sitting upright in the cart now. The employees made it a point to say hello and make conversation when they walked by. They respected Jack for being a good son and grandfather. When he passed, Lauren took over the role of corralling his two companions to the super store, and the first couple of outings were teary ones…The employees would voice their sorrows that turned into sobs.

Ellie got May home and deposited safely inside in the over-stuffed recliner that Edward Sr enjoyed watching football games in. "Well, I won't do that again!" proclaimed May. "I am so mad at myself. I knew better! "Both Ellie and May laughed.

Ellie knew that when summer came and May's shoulder was somewhat healed she would be out there cutting her own grass in ninety-degree weather. She liked it cut a certain way. Jack would receive numerous calls throughout the summer season from people driving by and seeing his elderly mother mowing her grass in the stifling heat. "Do you know your mother is out push-mowing her grass in this heat?" Jack would have to assure them that it was by her choice only. May would always say, "I would be happy if I dropped dead mowing my grass," which made people chuckle.

The next week started, and halfway through Jack came for a visit. He stayed for a couple of minutes. "I miss you all terribly and wish I were there with you." Lauren and Ellie voiced the same sentiments with teary eyes, and Jack finished the visit. "I love you all so much, and I will see you soon." Lauren looked at her mother with big puddles filling her pretty green eyes and said, "He seemed pretty sad. " Ellie thought that if they felt the struggle of communicating and living between two different worlds, so must Jack.

By the end of the week, at around midnight that Saturday, Lauren shuffled herself downstairs where her mother and Alexa were sleeping on the couch, and she leaned over and whispered. "He's here." Ellie's eyes flew open at those words. She jumped up and hustled into the dining room and took a seat. Ellie immediately asked Jack, "How are you?" She remembered the last visit. Jack said he was fine and that he had been spending more time with Mathews. "Mathews said he had a wife and her name was Calissa. He said he missed her vibrant smile." He continued. "He has come into the farmhouse a couple of times with me, but he can only enter with me and with my permission." There was something comforting to Ellie hearing that they both had each other on the other side. Mathews was stuck here on Earth, and Jack came and went from heaven, so Mathews's existence had to be lonely.

Ellie spoke up and asked, "What happened to his wife?"

Jack replied, "I don't know. He is a quiet man, and I let him talk without asking him too many questions so I don't offend him."

"Can you find out more information about his past next time you see him?"

Jack replied that he would…It was time to go.

Life kept the Westons busy with work, completing Lauren's house next door, and chasing the three babies. Ellie was fixing dinner one evening and she would glance over at the family room to watch Leo playing and acting goofy with the girls. All three of them were piling on top of him on the floor giggling and shrieking loudly as they jumped on him, and he made groaning noises like they were hurting him. Ellie thought back to when Lauren and Chance were that age. Jack would mow the grass with each one of them on either side of his lap, and the jostling of the mower would make them fall asleep. When Jack would turn the mower off and start to get off with them, they both would wake up and start crying. Then the process would start over again with Jack firing up the mower.

Jack was such a good father. He never missed a school function or sporting event and always made time for their children. Ellie just wished he was still here because he was just as good of a grandfather, and she worried that those three little girls would need him down the road . . . but he would be there waiting for them.

Ravine

Chapter Four
Ebb and Flow of Life

It was pretty quiet for several days, without a word from Jack. Ellie was missing him terribly. Even though he hadn't come forward lately, she knew he was always around. Lauren and Leo announced to Ellie that they were going to load the girls up and take them to Leo's parents for the evening to visit and eat dinner. Ellie knew they would be gone for a few hours so maybe she could watch a movie without interruption. Once they were gone she poured herself a glass of wine and threw some popcorn in the microwave. While she stood there and watched it pop, a smile came over her face. "Jack, how about a date night?" She assumed he had heard her, even though there was no response in return, and she got on with the evening.

Ellie grabbed her bowl of popcorn and headed to the couch with her cabernet sauvignon in hand and plopped down. After channel surfing a minute, she found a movie she had been wanting to see that was getting ready to start, so she settled herself in with a soft blanket and started sipping her wine. About halfway through the movie she thought Jack would be bored with the "chick flick," so she got up and strolled into the kitchen and poured herself another glass of wine before she headed up to the master bedroom.

If Jack was still there, Ellie knew what kind of "date night" Jack would want. She set her glass of wine down on the nightstand and went into her closet and stripped her clothes off. On the way to Jack's closet, she grabbed a bottle of perfume off the table that sat between the two closets and spritzed herself on her neck and wrist. Ellie walked into his closet and grabbed a blue and white small checkered dress shirt off the hanger and drew it to her face, smelling the hint of his cologne, even though it had been laundered and crisply ironed, and then she put it on.

Ellie left the shirt unbuttoned—after all, she still had a nice, toned body for a woman of her age—and walked over to the nightstand to light a candle, and she pulled out one of Jack's favorite adult toys he had purchased for her, and then she chugged the last few sips of her wine. Ellie hoped he enjoyed the evening as much as she did, but she was looking forward to hearing from him soon.

It took Jack a couple more days before he appeared again, and he seemed anxious when he did. "I have more information on Mathews." He said his first name is Tom, and his wife Calissa was pregnant and close to delivery when his parents beat her to death and then turned on him next. They tried to hang him first, but the noose broke, so when he hit the ground, they doused him with lamp oil and lit him on fire, then put the fire out and light him on fire all over again until he was dead. "

Ellie was so heartbroken to hear that parents could do that to their own child and grandchild, no matter the trespass they felt was done against them. Jack went on to tell them that Mathews said his parents were involved in unsavory illegal activity and that they felt he had married beneath them. Ellie's brain was on overdrive with the new information "Jack, can you see if he will show you where they were buried here on the farm and if he would mind if we put up some crosses to mark their graves?"

"I will see what I can find out."

Lauren said, "It's time for him to go."

"We love and miss you, Jack." Ellie always made it a point to tell him that she loved him before he left their visits. She felt she didn't say it enough when he was living.

It was already the first of February, and spring was just around the corner. Ellie was looking forward to working with Alexa in the flower/herb garden in front of the farmhouse. She loved to pull a sprig off of every herb and crush it in her tiny hands to release all the aroma, like her MiMi showed her, and smell it and identify them. Of course, her pronunciations were a little off sometimes.

Alexa also loved walking down past the barns to the big apple tree that was loaded with fruit and had branches hanging almost to the ground. She would pick her own apple and eat it on the way to the spring. There were large sandstone boulders that jutted out over the spring that ran twenty-four-seven all year round and put out a hundred gallons of water a minute. There was a large flat boulder next to the spring that Alexa liked to sit on and finish eating her apple while Ellie picked up sticks and pulled weeds around the pool of water the spring created.

When warmer weather hit, Ellie was also looking forward to watching Alexa drive the twins around in her battery-operated truck she and Jack had purchased for her last Christmas. She was too young to really use it then, but when Ellie saw it sitting on a shelf in the store, she asked Jack if he would mind if she returned the diamond earrings he had purchased for her so they could buy the truck, which was several hundred dollars.

Jack wanted her to keep the earrings too, but Ellie insisted on returning them. She was good at making money but also at saving it. Besides, she already had a couple pairs of nice diamond earrings that she rarely wore anyway.

Ellie knew that warm weather would also bring her son to the farm more often. Chance liked to trap shoot and ride four-wheelers out there with his buddies from work. He used to race four-wheelers, and he created practice tracks throughout the woods, which were also good for casualATV riding as well. The churning of the dirt on one of the used paths exposed a brown hand-thrown clay inkwell in pristine condition dating back to the early to mid-1800s that was found by Ellie. She couldn't believe it had survived harsh elements and even harsher thrashings from the four-wheelers, but it was now safe, sitting behind glass in a display cabinet in their farmhouse. Ellie was looking at it lately, wondering if it possibly belonged to Mathews.

Jack was starting to come more regularly now. He appeared the first Friday evening in February while Ellie and Lauren were sitting in the family room watching a movie. The girls had fallen asleep early that evening, and so did Leo. Jack never came through for a visit unless it was just Lauren and Ellie. He was always there observing. Alexa had on a few occasions since Jack passed shrieked with an excited voice and yell out, "There's PawPaw!" They knew she had caught sight of Jack. Whether that was intentional on his part or not, they weren't sure.

Lauren started to relay Jack's message. "I have a lot more information on Mathews. He said his parents were involved in sex trafficking of young innocent girls they would kidnap from all over, including that very county. They also sold harvested poppies and had some dealings with slaves. Mathews was an officer with the US Military. He did not approve of their lifestyle, and he turned his parents in and that is why they murdered him and his wife.

The room was silent for a minute after the delivery of the news. Ellie had to know more. She couldn't believe such a horrible event happened on their farm, no matter how long ago it was. "Jack, what was his parents' last name?" Ellie already knew that they didn't share the same last name because when the Westons bought the farm next door, they were given the abstract that dated back to 1816 when the United States first deeded the property to the first owner, and there was no owner after that with the last name of Mathews. He had also mentioned that his family owned the land going a half mile back and a couple of miles running along the road south of the farm. "I don't know. I will ask him."

"Mathews also said that after they were murdered, Calissa's parents fled to Connecticut with her younger sister to get away from all the evil and protect their youngest."

"Jack, that is terrible. It is hard to believe that such criminal activity took place back then and on this farm." Lauren continued to speak for Jack. "I know,

Ellie. I can show you this weekend where they are buried. The weather is supposed to be nice." Ellie nodded.

"It's time for me to go…I love you all."

Jack was gone.

•   •   •

Jack was on a roll. He appeared the next morning while the girls were in their high chairs eating their typical Saturday morning breakfast of pancakes and Leo was off to town with the trash. Lauren looked at Ellie and said, "He's here."

"Good Morning, Jack."

Ellie was glad he had made another appearance so soon. "I think you and Lauren should take a three-day holiday and relax," Jack said. He had overheard Lauren and Leo talking earlier that morning that Leo was going to be gone the third week in March to an archery shoot and his mother had agreed to watch all three girls.

Lauren spoke up. "Dad, I think that's a great idea." Ellie smiled and agreed.

Ellie had all night to ponder all that Jack had revealed to them yesterday. "Jack, do you think Mathews would come for a visit with you inside our home and speak with us?"

"I don't know. I will ask"

Ellie continued, "Will we be able to speak directly to him or see him?"

Jack replied, "I'm not sure, but I will be back in a couple of hours hopefully with Mathews, so I need to go now."

"Thanks, Jack. We love you and will talk to you soon." He was gone.

Ellie looked at Lauren and said, "I better get this house picked up." Ellie liked a tidy house and wanted it to always look its best for company . . . no matter if she could see them or not.

Within a couple hours, Ellie was finished with her mad-dash house cleaning, and as she walked back into the family room where Lauren was sitting… "Dad is on his way," Lauren announced. She would get vibes now, and as Jack got closer, the vibes would get stronger. She also told her mother she could now send a mental message to her father and he would come to her. "He's here."

Ellie asked, "Is he alone?"

"Dad says no. Mathews is with him, but I can't see him…Dad said to get something to write with." Ellie ran into the kitchen and grabbed a pen and small notebook out of their junk drawer and handed it to Lauren. Ellie started the conversation. "I guess we shouldn't be rude…Hello Mathews, thank you for coming."

Lauren said she could hear a man's voice mumbling to her father but couldn't make out the words. Ellie supposed it was part of the spirit world and that they weren't allowed to see or hear him. There were rules that had to be followed, according to Jack, or maybe that was Mathews just protecting himself from earthly beings. After all, his last experience on Earth was horrific and inflicted by someone who was supposed to protect him by natural instinct and unconditional love. No wonder there might be apprehension on his part.

Ellie watched Lauren look towards the chair closest to the patio doors and nod and then proceeded to write. Occasionally she would nod as she kept the pen in motion in acknowledgement that she had heard what Jack was telling her and writing it all down. Mathews had recounted the events of that tragic day through Jack with some additional information, and once he was done, Lauren handed the notebook to her mother and said, "Read."

As Ellie started to read, Lauren said, "Mathews says it's hard to talk about."

Ellie looked up from the writing and looked in the direction of the chair and said, "It is hard to hear and read what happened to you and, we are so sorry."

Lauren repeated what Jack was relaying. "His wife Calissa was twenty-three years old and taught kids in the area." Ellie took it as she was a teacher. "He saw her for a brief time in heaven but she went on and he chooses to stay at the farm. It is peaceful here, and he loves it." Ellie wasn't sure what kind of strain the brutal killings put on their marital relationship in the afterlife but thought there had to be some sort of resentment and guilt by both. Ellie didn't want to ask too many questions on his first visit because she wanted him to come back.

Ellie continued to direct her questions to Mathews. "So you can go to heaven but choose to stay here?"

"Yes, it is peaceful, and I am not sure if I went back to heaven I would see my wife now. We had a little girl…Babies continue to grow in heaven up to the size where they still have their innocence. She will be forever around the toddler age . . . three years old. We both liked the name Matilda."

"Mathews I worry about you being lonely here on Earth."

He replied, "I'm not. I have Jack." That made Ellie well up with so much pride. Even on the other side he was still trying to be the peacekeeper. She smiled really big and said, "Jack is a great guy."

Mathews responded, "Yes he is."

Ellie then said, "I understand that you used to sleep in the sugar shack we tore down?"

"Yes." Ellie was her usual self, wanting to fix things for people. "Well, I think we are going to have to remedy that."

Ellie remembered that she would walk into the old three-sided shack while it was still standing and get the feeling that something slept there. She thought it was coyotes. Little did she know. Makes sense to her now. It was dry, had old bales of hay in there . . . and was rustically cozy.

Lauren spoke up and said, "Dad says that Mathews has to go now. He doesn't have as much time as Dad." More rules.

Ellie finished. "Mathews, we are glad you came today, and we love you Jack." They were gone.

Lauren said, "Dad sent me a message as he was leaving. He will be back tomorrow afternoon to show us where Mathews and Calissa were buried.

•   •   •

Jack kept his word. He was back the next day around 4:00 P.M. Ellie had been outside with Alexa all day collecting leaves and picking up sticks and limbs from past storms. It was an unusually warm day for February, registering sixty degrees, which was great for yardwork and taking a walk into the woods.

Lauren had already changed into her jeans and hiking boots when Ellie and Alexa entered the house. "He's on his way. Let's go ahead and walk on out to the deck." Ellie was amazed that Jack could telepathically send Lauren messages now, and vice versa. "He's arrived." Ellie followed Lauren with Alexa perched on her mother's shoulders, and they walked to the open area where the sugar shack used to sit, veered right, walked about a hundred feet, and then headed north into the woods ten feet, and they were there.

"Dad says they are buried in this area inside these four small trees," Ellie pulled out the twine and cut four sections off and tied them to the branches so they could come back and dig until they found a shoe, button, bone, or something that would indicate that it was the exact spot so it would never be disturbed and so she could place inconspicuous markers. After Ellie tied the last piece of twine, she turned around in the direction of the open field and the vista beyond and thought, *What a beautiful view. No wonder Mathews thought the farm was special too.*

Ellie asked Lauren, "Is your dad still with us?"

"No, he left already, but we will see him soon."

"Mom, do you want to walk to the spring?"

"Yes, that's a great idea, and I can take some pictures of you and Alexa sitting on the big boulder." Alexa let out a little squeal…She thought that sounded like a good idea. She wasn't ready to go inside yet.

The work week was off to another start for Ellie. She knew she had to work a couple of late evenings that week, but the real estate market was still a little slow, which allowed her to work on other things. Ellie and Lauren decided they were going to have a barn sale out at the farm and open it up to other vendors, food trucks, and even a band. They both loved antiques and handmade items. Ellie thought this would be a great way to bring in more income for the farm and her family.

The first couple of days of the week were pretty quiet around the farm. Lauren had taken Alexa to dance class on Tuesday with the twins in hand. Afterward she was meeting one of her girlfriends for dinner. Ellie wasn't sure how much girl talk they would be able to do with three little ones with them, but Lauren had gone to high school with Kayla and knew she was pretty laid back so she could handle the interruptions.

On the way home, Lauren called her mother and said she felt seizure-sick and that Jack was in the car with her. Ellie quickly asked if she needed her to come pick her and the girls up, but Lauren assured her that she could make it home. She told her mother she was only three miles from the farm. Leo was home, so he helped Lauren get the girls inside and changed for bed. It was already 9:00 P.M. Lauren said goodnight to her mother and headed for her bed. Ellie hoped she would be able to fight off a seizure. Lauren had been seizure-free for almost three months.

Ellie was going through her morning routine with dogs, laundry, emptying the dishwasher, and helping with Alexa, when Lauren came into the kitchen and said, "We have company this morning. Good morning Jack, how are you?"

Jack got straight to the point of his visit. "Dad is telling me the reason I feel seizure-sick is because other spirits are trying to reach out to me now, the word is out in the spirit world. There are others that were murdered on the farm that want to speak with me and need our help."

Just when Ellie thought she couldn't be surprised anymore by what they were experiencing…She was proven wrong.

"Dad is asking if you can come back home today between 12:30 and 1:30 P.M. He wants to bring Mathews and let him tell you about the others."

Ellie answered, "Of course I will be here."

Jack said, "I better go now and will see you a little later…I love you both."

Ellie arrived at work and immediately got the day started addressing messages and confirming appointments for later on in the day. Once she had the obligatory calls finished, she glanced at the time on her computer. There was another hour before she needed to leave. She was anxious to hear all that Mathews had to tell them. The time seemed to creep by until the noon hour popped up in the corner of her screen. She headed back to the farm.

Ellie walked into the farmhouse and Lauren was in the family room with the twins in their highchairs and Alexa running about, occasionally glancing up at the cartoons on the TV. The sitter was ill and Lauren was home with the girls. Mi Mi said hello to all the girls, took her coat off, and draped it over the couch. "They are ready to talk Mom. Take a seat." Ellie quickly grabbed a pen and notebook from the kitchen counter. She tried to leave them handy now so she could make a record of all that was said.

When Ellie sat down, she acknowledged they were there. "Hello Jack and Mathews." She turned to Lauren and asked, "Can you see Mathews?" Lauren nodded in the affirmative.

The conversation took off at a fast pace, with Mathews pouring out what he knew. "There are other spirits here that would like to come forward and meet Lauren and get your help so they can move on.

Ellie replied, "We are here to help."

Mathews continued with the information. "There is a little boy here on the farm. His name is Benton, and he is eight years old. I am not sure what happened to him…I have also met a father and daughter. His name is James and his nine-year-old daughter's name is Felicia. Felicia was taken by runners of my parents' child sex trafficking operation, and her father came looking for her. He found her here on the farm, and my parents told him if he took one more step on their property, they were going to kill her…He took another step. Some of the runners were told to hold him down and make him watch while the other runners raped his little girl, and when they were done, they shot her and then shot and killed him too. Their bodies were thrown in a ravine next to a sink hole."

Ellie was fighting back tears after hearing about the monstrous things that had taken place on their beautiful farm. It must be hard for Mathews to admit his own parents were at the head of it. Ellie said, "Yes, I think I know the location you are talking about." She had walked every square inch of the woods on the farm with the dogs. "Can you show us the exact location?"

Lauren answered for him. "Yes, and he says we will find other items of interest there."

Mathews continued. "There is also a bag with evidence buried here on the farm."

Ellie quickly inquired, "Can you also take us to that location?"

"I believe so. The farm was finally raided after a girl was taken from a prominent family that had some power. There were small shacks that were built everywhere on the farm that housed the runners and the young victims. They were torn down and burned." Ellie was curious. "Who organized the raid . . . authorities? Neighbors and families that fell victim?" Mathews said he didn't know. He was already dead…Ellie wasn't sure how he came about that particular piece of information but felt bad for asking. "There were other children that perished along the journey to the farm, and they would discard their little bodies like trash. Sometimes they fell ill and sometimes they suffered at the hands of the runners," he said.

Ellie kept letting the questions fly out. If he was willing to answer them, she would keep after the truth. "What was your mother's name?"

"Mary Ellen was her first name, but I don't know what my stepfather's last name was. When I was seventeen, my biological father went missing, and I went looking for him only to find out they murdered him. I left the farm after that. I lived elsewhere for three years before I returned to the county."

"I was an officer in the U. S. Army, and I also worked for the town of Stenson."

There was a long pause, then Ellie went on with the questioning. "How could such a big child sex trafficking organization carry on beyond the reach of the law?"

Mathews answered, "Because there was corruption at all levels of authority in the county, from the judge, JPs, and other influential folks in the area. Some neighbors turned a blind eye to it and others were also involved."

Ellie knew there had to be others in the area that knew what was going on at the farm—especially the authorities. After all, it was a small town and people talked.

Mathews directed his question to Lauren. "Is it okay to bring others forward to you once they trust us?"

Lauren responded, as Ellie knew she would, "Of course. We are here to help." Mathews said thank you and that they needed to go for now but would be back.

Ellie hated to see them go. "We love you, Jack, and Matthewss, you are part of our family now." "Thank you, Ellie. It's been a long time since I had a family."

They were gone. . . .

Lauren and Ellie looked at each other in amazement. Ellie was so proud of her family for pulling together to help those other spirits. This all started with Jack on the other side making friends with Mathews and earning his trust…Typical Jack.

Ellie had to get back to work and finish the day with her last two appointments, and then she was off to dinner with Chance and Mia. They were dining at the clubhouse on the golf course where they used to live. Ellie so wished she could tell her son what all had taken place lately on the farm and what all had taken place in the past, but she knew better, Chance did not share her beliefs about life on the other side of this one.

The next morning, Ellie was getting ready for work when Lauren called up the stairs to her mother. "Can you please come here?" Ellie immediately stopped putting on her makeup and raced down the stairs with Alexa on her hip. Every morning Alexa would help organize all the makeup with her little hands and then insist her Mi Mi put some on her as well.

Lauren said, "We have company."

Ellie inquired, "Is your father alone?"

"No, he has Mathews with him and a little boy named Benton." Ellie quickly acknowledged everyone and made special effort to say, "Hello Benton. We are glad you came today."

Mathews relayed all to Lauren. "Mathews says Benton wanted to come forward and tell you his story and all that he saw took place here, so he can move on when he is ready." Mathews kept talking on Benton's behalf. "He was eight years old when he was murdered. He was forced to stand watch over the other children that were locked in big cages inside the shacks. Benton befriended a little girl from France. She was nine years old and spoke both French and English. He would play cards with her to keep her entertained. There were also two smaller children running freely in the shack.

"One-night Benton decided he wanted to try to save them. First he loaded one of the toddlers in a wheelbarrow and covered her up and wheeled her out of sight to the underbrush by the creek bed. Benton's job was to remove the buckets of waste from the children's shacks, and he used the wheelbarrow to do it. He hoped he would go unnoticed by the runners. After he got her safely deposited, he went back for the other small child. He was halfway to the creek bed with the wheelbarrow with the other child when he was caught and shot on the right side of his head. He wasn't sure what happened to the other children he was trying to save, but he guessed they met the same fate.

"He was shot by his parents. They were the ones operating the child trafficking." Benton and Mathews had the same mother and Mathews' stepfather was Benton's biological father.

Mathews said, "I didn't realize he was my brother!" Ellie and Lauren didn't quite have all the information sometimes, mainly because Ellie would be so intent on listening to what was being relayed to them. They would get bits and pieces later. It was her understanding that Mathews was aware that there were a couple of children spirits on the farm, but from what she gathered, everyone kept to themselves. They all left this world under the hands of evil people so who could blame them for not trusting on the other side?

Benton told Mathews he wasn't afraid to die and that he needed to try and help those other children. How could two sweet souls have been born from a womb belonging to the evilest woman Ellie had ever heard tell of?

Ellie spoke up. "Benton we are so proud of you and you are such a brave boy. Don't be afraid to move on to heaven. It is a safe place, and you will be loved there."

Mathews then spoke through Lauren. "He is going to stay with me a while longer. He didn't realize he had family." That made Ellie smile as tears ran down her face.

Ellie really hadn't spoken to Jack the last couple of visits. "Jack, how are you doing?" Lauren spoke for him. "Fine, just heartbroken." Ellie nodded. She knew what he was talking about. All those that were abused and murdered at the hands of those monsters. "Dad says they have to go now but there will be more children spirits that will be coming forward." Ellie and Lauren both nodded. Andrews had one more thing to say. "I can show you where Benton is also buried." Before they all left, Ellie said, "I am so proud of you Jack, and I love you even more, and Mathews and Benton thank you for coming and you are both family now, and we love you too."

Jack had one more thing to say before they left. "Lauren, you need to leave the house with your mother today." They all could feel someone trying to come through and it wasn't someone wanting help but someone menacing…possibly someone that didn't want all the terrible secrets out of what happened there. Ellie and Lauren agreed to leave at the same time…They were gone.

After they left, Ellie asked Lauren to describe what Benton looked like. "He has the same sandy-colored hair that Mathews has, green eyes, and a big scar on the right side of his temple."

Ellie helped Lauren get the girls dressed and out the door to start their day, even though they had more important work there at the farm. Ellie still had bills to pay and clients to take care of.

The workday came and went and Ellie was able to make it home by five o'clock that evening, which was early for her. She wanted to get as much done as she could because Jack's visits were picking up to sometimes two and three times a day now. There were so many little ones that needed their help, and Ellie and Lauren were more than happy to help.

Jack made a quick appearance a couple hours after Ellie arrived home. Lauren ran into the kitchen and said, "I need a piece of paper and pen. Dad is here and he has names and ages of little girls that died here." Lauren flipped open the notepad and names and ages started to fill the lines:

Rene', age seven; Macey, age five; Janelle, age nine; Estelle, age nine; Stella, age four; Bessie, age six; Margaret, age five; Elizabeth, age ten.

"Dad said he will be back later tonight; there is a little girl wanting to tell us what happened to her and then she will move on to Heaven. He also said to protect those names on the paper and keep it out of sight. He loves us… He's gone."

Ellie looked at the piece of paper Lauren had written the names on. There were eight so far, and they were so young. Ellie couldn't believe such evil could come to such innocence. How could so many people look the other way, no matter how much money and influence those people had?

The evening's needs made Lauren and Ellie get back to bathing babies, doing laundry, and all the other daily chores. Leo had finally made it home from a late workday and played a few minutes with the girls before he helped Lauren put the twins down in their cribs upstairs, and Ellie and Alexa got situated on the couch. Ever since Jack had passed Alexa didn't like sleeping upstairs, so Ellie didn't force the issue. She knew Alexa was also missing her papaw.

Ellie dozed off, but as soon as she heard Lauren's shuffling down the stairs, she popped up and grabbed the notebook to take notes. "Dad is here with a little girl. Her name is Sadie, and she was nine when they murdered her.

"The runners had taken her from her family. She came from up north somewhere." Lauren continued to repeat Sadie. "She said she was labeled a 'prime girl' because she was still a virgin, but on the journey to the farm one of the runners raped her. Once she arrived, she was considered of no value to them, so they sexually assaulted her and then beat her to death with a stone."

Ellie spoke up. "We are so sorry for what happened to you."

Sadie said, "Thank you. Things happen for a reason." Ellie thought there was no reason why something so heinous should have happened to those children. "I can move on now." She was gone.

Jack was still there. "Jack how are you doing?" Ellie knew this was also hard on him.

"I am tired, but I am picking up the grandfather role for these kids. They need me."

Ellie smiled. "Thank you for taking such good care of them, and we love you." Jack said he would be back tomorrow…He was gone.

●　　●　　●

It was the next morning and Ellie had already taken a shower and was tending to Alexa when Lauren came into the family room and said, "Dad will be here shortly." within a minute she said, "They are here."

Ellie wasn't sure who all came through. "Is Mathews with him?"

Lauren replied yes.

"Is Benton with them?"

"No, but a little girl came, and Dad said she is deaf."

Ellie was so thankful that Lauren had been learning sign language lately. Before Jack passed, Lauren had ordered a self-teaching sign language book, and when Jack came through on one of his first visits, he had told Lauren to learn to sign. Looking back now, Ellie can see that that was probably a message from a higher place. Even Jack probably didn't know why he was to relay that message to Lauren and how important it would be for Lauren to heed that advice.

The little girl started the conversation with her hands. "I am ten years old. My name is Grace. I was taken from my family and brought to the farm. When they realized I couldn't speak they hung me. They thought I had mental issues because I couldn't talk."

Lauren signed back to her. "We are so sorry, and we love you very much." The little girl was gone; she moved on.

Jack and Mathews were still there. Ellie asked, "Is Benton still with you Mathews?"

He replied, "Yes, he will be with me for a while."

Ellie voiced, "I am so happy you have each other."

Jack said it was time to go. "I love you, and I will be back."

Ellie said she loved him and thanked him for all that he was doing. She knew he had to be tired mentally and physically. Ellen and Lauren were about to head out the door for work when Lauren turned to her mother. "Wait, I am getting vibes."

Ellie stood still for a minute. "Dad's here and he has Benton with him. He said Benton has something to tell us."

Ellie spoke to Benton. "Good morning Benton." Lauren began relaying what Benton wanted to say. "Thank you for helping us. I have never really had a family before." Ellie smiled and said, "You are so welcome, and we are so proud of you for being such a brave boy. We love you and your brother and you are now part of our family."

Ellie was glad Benton came this morning because she still needed to know what his father's last name was. "Benton do you know what your father's last name was?"

"No, I had to call him Sir or Thomas and wasn't allowed to call him father. I had to raise myself and then was forced to work and do what I was told." Ellie nodded in acknowledgement.

Lauren then said, "Dad says they have to go and he might come to work with us, if he has the energy today." Ellie said her goodbyes to them both… They were gone.

Jack didn't appear that day, but he was back that evening to say they would be there in the morning with more little ones. Ellie was so upset pouring over the notes she had taken earlier. "How could someone do those things to another person, Jack? Especially a child?"

Jack replied, "I don't know Ellie, but the stories don't get any better." Some of the children spirits wanted to be escorted directly to heaven and escape all that happened to them. Jack and Matthews were more than happy to oblige.

But some of them wanted the living to know what had happened. they had been waiting so long to be set free…some almost two hundred years.

• • •

For the next two weeks, both children and adult spirits kept coming through with Jack and Mathews escorting them to tell their horrendous stories of what took place on the farm so long ago:

- Elsey, age ten: She came from another country by ship. Her parents were struggling financially so they sent her to live with her aunt and uncle, and they traveled to the U. S. She had a younger brother that stayed behind with their parents. Once they got off the ship, it was chaotic, and she got separated from them and that's when the runners took her. It was terrible there on the farm. Some children were housed in tents and some in the shacks. "We only had empty feed sacks to cover us to try and keep warm."

They were given dirty water to drink—usually their bath water—even though there was plenty of fresh spring water, and were fed dry corn and a little bread most of the time. Some children would eat grass because they were so hungry, and it would make their belly bloat. She could remember one good meal she was fed. They usually fed a child that was sold and getting ready to leave the farm a decent meal before they shipped them off. Sometimes they were fed other children…

It was super cold when she arrived, and she had developed frostbite on her feet. They turned black, so they cut her legs off. There was no medicine. "I still had value since I was pretty and could still be sold. They didn't like my temper so one day they snapped my neck and killed me."

- Rene', age seven: The living conditions were bad. The prettier you were the better they treated you. I became ill, so they starved me and put me outside of the shack until I died.

- Cali, age six: She came through with Mathews and Jack but didn't want to say what happened; she just wanted to visit. She watched Alexa laugh and run around her weaving in and out of the curtains on the patio doors in the family room.

- Joseph, age thirteen: He was kidnapped from his family in broad daylight. They traveled four to five hours by horse to get there. He managed to survive for two years there on the farm. Once a week they would drag sick kids out of the shacks and kill and burn them. There were always fires burning on the farm. The runners had to rape some of the little girls to prove their loyalty. He refused…and was shot.

- Annalise, age sixteen: Brown, curly hair and green eyes. She met the people that had bought her, and when they traveled away from the farm, she escaped and ran back to the farm. The people came back for her and killed her on the spot.

- Katie, age twelve, and Jessie, age seven, sisters: They were kidnapped together and wanted to stay together. They were to be sold separately, and when the girls refused to be separated, they were tortured and beaten with stones…They died a couple of days later.

- Abigail, age fifteen: She lived in the same county. In the middle of the night she was kidnapped by the runners, and her family was tied up in their house, and then they burned it to the ground. She was here a couple of months. When she hit puberty, she became useless to them. They starved her, and when she became unconscious, they beat her to death. She was tall and had a slender build with strawberry blonde hair and blue eyes.

- Levin, age thirteen, and Bristol, age eleven, brother and sister: Her brother was turned into a runner and they were both murdered there. When the organization tried to force them to have sexual intercourse with each other, they said no, so they were killed. Bristol hasn't seen her brother since then and thinks he moved on to heaven. Some of the children stayed there on the farm after they were murdered, just waiting for their parents to find them and be reunited.

- Georgina, age thirteen: She fell in love with a runner, and they were trying to run away but they were caught by an older couple, and they tried to say they were running to get exercise, but they didn't believe them and they were hanged together. She was taken from her home at age eleven. She had lived on the farm for two years. She had been there the longest. Her parents sold her to them. They lived a couple of miles from there. Not all the children were kidnapped; some were actually sold by their parents.

- Bea, age six: Brutally raped…She bled out and died.

- Davida age ten: She lasted three days on the farm. She got confrontational with a runner, and he accused her of using witchcraft against him. They hanged her.

- Twins Maliah and Ariel, age nine: They were kidnapped from their bedroom in the middle of the night. The runners put something in their eyes so they couldn't see very well for a couple of days. It took two days and two nights to travel to the farm. It was auction time, and they split the girls up and they each were sold to different men. As Maliah was being loaded into the buggy she jumped out and the man grabbed her arm which caused her to catch on something sharp on the buggy and her arm to be severely cut. It hit an artery and bled out quickly, and she died, so the men argued over Ariel, and she was in between them and was accidentally shot and killed.

(The girls said they would take berries and use them to make the girls up before auction, and if a girl was coming into puberty sometimes they would inject her breast area with animal fat (cow or pig) to help her sell better, but the girls would then die soon after from infections.)

- Kristin, age nine: They kept her blindfolded most of the time. One day they came to her shack and clubbed her to death. She could hear her bones cracking.

- Lucy, age four: She was traumatized from being taken from her parents and she kept soiling herself. The wife sewed her anus shut for punishment for a few days. The "nurse" took out the stitches without permission to help to heal her. The organization felt she was of no value, so they sewed her eyes and mouth shut, hog-tied her, and let her be raped by anyone wanting to. After they did that to her, they left her tied up and threw her in the woods to die and be eaten by wild animals.

- Amera, age five: She kept wanting to ride a horse, and it angered the runners, so they stabbed her to death.

- Johnny, age eleven: Was a runner's son. He was run over by a carriage after witnessing another boy being dragged to his death by a horse. He didn't elaborate on why he was murdered.

- Hannah, age fifteen: She was kidnapped by runners. She was married to Jevin, age twenty-seven. They lived across the river just a few miles away. The owners kept her blindfolded in a shack with no windows most of the time. Her husband came looking for her and was yelling her name. She called back, and they dragged her out of the shack. Jevin explained that they were married and were expecting a child, so they slit open her stomach then shot her and then shot her husband.

- Anna and Claire, age nine: They were playing in Anna's yard when they were taken by runners. They both lived in the county. One of the runners accused them of witchcraft and they burned both of them on a stake.

- Bryson, age eight: He was kidnapped from his family by runners. He was supposed to be sold for the purpose of sex, but before they did, the runners thought he needed to be broken in, so several of them took their turn at him. He became physically ill (vomiting) from the pain. He became angry and fought back, so they killed him.

- Annisa, age eight: She was the first girl to arrive on the farm. She had been kidnapped from her parents. There was only one shack, and they were starting to build more. She had some freedom to walk around with an overseer and would walk down to the spring, until she tried to run away, then they starved her. She would cry because she was so hungry, and they would tell her to be quiet. She started biting the other children, so they hanged her as an example to the others.

- Mitton, age thirteen: Forced to be a runner, he was there on the farm for one to two months and was poisoned and died in 1832.

- Gretta, age fifteen: She was kidnaped from northern Indiana while walking home from a shop and then brought to the farm. She was there for two months. She was planning her escape and telling her eight-year-old shack mate what she was doing and that she was leaving at midnight. When she walked out of the shack, the runners were waiting for her and asked if she was ready to run away. They tied her hands behind her back and told her to start running. The last thing she heard was one of them yell attack, and six large dogs chased her down and mauled her to death; it was over in a couple of minutes. She said that you never saw or heard the dogs on the farm, but they were there.

- "Feisty Tom Boy," age sixteen: Didn't want to give her name. She made it on the farm about a year. Some of the older children were made to empty the waste buckets, and some were made to wash the clothes of children that died or were murdered so they could be reused. She liked doing manual labor, so she took care of the poppies. She also liked chewing tobacco. One of the runners would share his tobacco with her because she let him touch her for payment…They were caught. Her punishment was a brutal rape by many until she became unconscious from the pain and damage. They buried her alive. She lived for ten minutes before suffocating to death. If anyone finds her necklace with a golden heart locket, she would like it back.

- "Girl," age five: She was so traumatized from what happened to her, she doesn't remember her name. She had dark-brown, wavy hair and was very pretty. There was a bidding war over her, and the men became aggressive…They all wanted her. She started to cry and tried to run off, but a runner held her with a knife to her throat. She had seen several children being brutally raped and murdered there on the farm so she understood how things were most likely going to end for her, so she threw her head towards the knife, severing an artery in her neck, and she bled to death.

There were others that met a brutal death besides the children:

- Deidre, age twenty-seven, a nurse: She woke up one day there at the farm not sure how she got there. She was either knocked unconscious or drugged. She was made to be a "nurse" taking care of sick children and examining the girls when they arrived there to verify that they were still virgins. The girls would beg her to lie if they were raped along the journey by a runner because if their virginity wasn't still intact, they would be raped and murdered. Thomas, the owner of the organization, made Deidre call him daddy, and he raped her many times until she became pregnant. Once his wife noticed she was showing, she pressed her, wanting to know who impregnated her, and Deidre lied and said one of the workers, but he denied it and the truth came out.

They tied her down and stomped on her stomach until the baby was aborted. It was a boy. He was about twenty weeks and very small. They gave her a couple days, then Thomas's wife came back and sewed her vagina closed. Deidre said she felt humiliated. Then she cut off her hair so Deidre would look like a man and then cut off her breasts. Deidre was forced to continue working. She lasted twelve days until an infection set in and killed her. The more you made the owners mad, the worse your death. A bullet was kind.

(Some children were sold by their parents to the trafficking organization for drugs. The drugs that were sold were poppies to eat and salvia to smoke.)

- Phoena age twenty-nine: Her son Ben, age seven, saw his sister Maddie, age five, being taken out of their yard by two men. They had searched for her for a week when Ben caught sight of one of the men on the horse path, so they followed him to the farm. It was only twenty minutes from their home. Pheona had him hide in the tall grass along the creek bed and rode in on horse by herself. She saw the owners and said she wanted her daughter back, and they told her no. She politely left and planned to come back at night to rescue her. She sent Ben to her parents a few miles away and went back that night to the farm…She was caught by a runner, and he drowned her in a bucket of water. When she didn't return three days later, her parents took Ben and left the area; they knew her fate. Her husband was off fighting in a war when it all happened and they never saw him again. Jack and Mathews were able to find her daughter, and they were now reunited on the farm.

- Jeremy, age twenty-nine: He was a runner. His family was starving, and he took a job with the organization. He didn't do anything bad to the little girls; he only had to pick them up from their parents that sold or traded them to the organization. He had a wife and a daughter. When his daughter was four years old, another runner caught sight of her, and they kept watch until she turned seven. They had decided to take her, but Jeremy heard about their plan and raced home to send his wife and daughter off before the runners got there and took her from them. He was successful, but he never saw his family again. The runners caught up with him and dragged him back to the farm, and they murdered him by taking a large stone and beating him in the head.

- Frederick, age thirty-seven, and Jonathan, age seventeen; Father and son: Jonathan's wife Samantha, age sixteen, went missing in the middle of the night after she went to go check on a horse birthing a foal. They lived twenty minutes away, and when they realized she had been taken, they decided to see if she was there. When they made it to the farm, they inquired about her and were taken captive. Their hands tied behind their backs, and an elderly man put on a black hood and hanged them both. After they spoke, they were moving onto heaven because they couldn't find her.

- Robert Martan, age forty-four, foreman on the farm: It was 1852, and he was working undercover for parents to save their children under the premise that he wanted to take over the business one day. In all, he saved thirty-seven girls until he was caught. He would have kids fake their death, and then he would carry them into the woods as if he was going to throw them in the ravine, but he would keep walking through the woods and be met by the child's parents, and they were saved. He would also try to get them clean water from the spring and take care of any wounds they had; the children called him their guardian angel. He worked on the farm for nine months.

When he was caught, they took a metal ball and shoved it in his mouth (which broke many teeth) to silence the torture they were going to put him through. First, they cut off his toes and fingers and then his ears, and next they tied him to a tree and let others hit and kick him until he fell unconscious, only to bring him back to consciousness by lighting him on fire. He said it was worth going through all of that to save those girls.

Just when Ellie thought she couldn't hear a worse story than the one before, another spirit showed up to tell it. Robert continued, "There is a brown leather bag containing a ledger with all the girl's names and ages, if they were sold and for how much, or if they died. It is located at the back of the property to the left of the roadway before you hit the woods. I doubt that it has survived this long in the ground because it is a wet area back there." Ellie asked Jack and Mathews if they could show her where it is. Jack spoke up. "Yes, we will show you." It was one more location for her to dig up the unspeakable past, but it needed to be done.

Jack spoke up and said, "The reason that people didn't pay much attention to the farm as they passed by was the owners were working under the pretense that they were running an orphanage and helping place children that had no families." That made complete sense to Ellie, why no one pressed them for information and why the authorities were able to look the other way without too much ridicule.

"There was also a secret society that knew what horrible things could and would be done to the children, and they were more than happy to purchase them and participate. I am trying to find out more about that." Lauren relayed that it was time for them to go. "I love and miss you both terribly." They were gone.

Things on Jack's end started to get weird. When he came through the next time he seemed anxious. "There is chaos here and Mathews and I don't know why. We are trying to figure it out."

Ellie was concerned. "What do you mean, Jack?"

He answered, "The sky got really dark as far as you could see, and the wind was roaring. We had to tie ropes around our waists and tether ourselves to trees." That sounded ominous to Ellie, like it might be angry spirits. Whatever the cause, she knew that Jack and Mathews would get to the bottom of things.

It was quiet for a couple of days and Ellie was nervous that they might have lost contact with Jack for good, but he came one evening. Lauren had just gotten the twins down, and when she walked into the kitchen, she said the sweetest words to Ellie's ears. "Dad's here."

"Hello Jack, what did you find out?"

Jack seemed more at ease. "The dark sky and wind was caused by other spirits here on the farm. There are quite a few spirits out there that don't know who we are yet, and it made them nervous, but things have calmed down for now. I think there were a lot more people murdered out here than what we first thought…Hundreds of children."

Ellie spoke next. "Jack, I know this has been hard on all of us, but we all need to stay positive and strong and we will get through this."

Lauren answered for Jack. "Yes, I agree." "Jack I need you to show me the exact location of the ledger this weekend. It is supposed to quit raining by the first of the week, and Chance is going to bring his excavator out here and we are going to start unearthing things. I have not told him what I am doing, just that I want to work on the ravine that previous owners had dumped items into over the years"…There were some old tires, pieces of old barn, old canning jars, and whatever lied beneath that." She was hoping to find clues to the past. Jack agreed. "I will show you and Lauren so we can continue to help those that are still here."

Jack went on. "Do you have any more questions?"

Ellie inquired, "How's Mathews? He hasn't been with you the last couple of times?"

"He has really been helping me, I'm sure he will come with me on the next visit. I love you both, but I better get back. Lots to do."

"We love you Jack and we will see you soon."

He was gone…

Ellie became obsessed with finding out who the owners of the organization were, but it was proving difficult. Every time they spoke with a spirit no one knew the last name, and Mathews thought they kept changing their names anyway to hide their identities, as that was easy to do back then with no way to verify identification. In between appointments Ellie started to meet with the town historians there in Stenson looking for any information on crime back at that time and any information they had on her beloved farm that she still adored.

The next few days were pretty uneventful at the farm. Jack and Mathews would come by and visit, and slowly Ellie would get more personal information out of Mathews. When he served in the US Army, he worked the coastlines helping to map out the territories. He told them interesting things like, they knew marijuana could get you high back then so the soldiers would use the barrel of their rifles and fill it with gun powder and marijuana, burn it, and then inhale the smoke, and for constipation they would eat lard. Mathews had also become intrigued by a popular mini-series on TV that takes place a few hundred years AC about rulers conquering other kingdoms and claiming new territories. The TV was always on in the Weston house. Ellie wasn't sure what Mathews did with all his time before meeting Jack and becoming part of their family, but she was sure he was learning new things all the time, especially new words and terminology. On a couple of visits, Jack had to act as interpreter for everyone, but Mathews was a quick study.

Toward the end of that week, Jack and Mathews came and said they had someone that would like to come forward, so of course Lauren and Ellie agreed to speak with them. Much to Ellie's surprise, they had found Mathews' biological father, Teddy. When he came forward, he explained that a strange man had moved into the area and had caught the attention of his wife Mary Ellen, Mathews' mother, so she divorced him and took Mathews to live with her and her new man, Thomas. A few years passed, and then they purchased the farm which adjoined Teddy's property that laid beyond the spring, and that's when they started their child sex-trafficking operation.

When Teddy realized what was going on, he tried to get his son away from them, and they murdered him. He said his wife just laughed while he was being tortured. He couldn't understand why she had turned into such a horrible person; they had a good life. Teddy was a veterinarian and made good money since horses were the mode of transportation at that time.

After he told his story, he was ready to leave. Ellie spoke up. "Thank you for coming Teddy, and we are so happy that you and Mathews have each other again. Lauren and Ellie were glad that Mathews' existence just kept getting better . . . first becoming best friends with Jack, then meeting a brother he didn't realize he had, and now reuniting with his father. The first two hundred years must have been so lonely, but things were looking up for Mathews.

The week's weather was typical for the time of year; it was still raining and snowing, so there was no digging yet, but things started to pick up again in the spirit world. Jack showed up one evening and said he hadn't seen Mathews for a couple of hours. Children started panicking and running to the other side of the dome of spirit world, so he followed them to see what had frightened them. Ellie told Jack, "I am sure he will come back and all will be fine." Lauren said her father was nervous. Jack stayed for about an hour sitting in a chair just watching his family with the evening goings-on without saying much, and Ellie finally got brave enough to throw out an idea she had been thinking about. "You know, when the spirit children come through to tell their story, they seem to be mesmerized by cartons on TV, so I was thinking that we need to occasionally have a movie night on the farm and invite all the spirits. I will buy a big outdoor projection screen, and we can get some children-appropriate movies. What do you think?" Lauren piped up and thought that was a super idea, and Jack was smiling so big, according to his daughter, and he added, "You can bring out the cotton candy machine, popcorn machine, and the snow cone machine. Ellie you will need to get one of the blow-up screens for that." She wasn't sure what he was talking about but assured him that they would research what equipment they would need to purchase to pull it off. Jack also threw out, "and maybe get a kegerator for the adults. Lauren has been wanting one.

Ellie agreed that was all a great idea and was making a mental note of the family friends they would invite for the movie premieres, of course, without mentioning the attendance of their special guests.

Suddenly Jack said he needed to go, that something needed his attention, but he would be back.

Lauren and Ellie kept up with their evening chores, and Ellie slipped upstairs with the vacuum and was going from room to room until she made it to the master bedroom. She unplugged the vacuum so she could plug it into another outlet when Lauren called up softly, "You need to come down here." Ellie didn't hesitate. She rounded the corner into the kitchen, and Lauren said, "Dad is back and he found Mathews. When you were upstairs vacuuming you scared a spirit and it came down here. It was black, and it poked its head around the corner and looked at me three times and took off into the dining room."

Jack started explaining all that he found out. "The black spirit was a runner, and the children caught sight of him because they recognized him and they panicked and started running, but Mathews assured them that he can't hurt them ever again. In fact, Mathews and I chased him off and told him not to come back." Ellie was concerned to hear that but was not frightened by his presence…After all, he was dead. What she couldn't understand is why he wasn't in hell, where he belonged? But she would get her answer the next morning.

Before Jack left the visit, he said, "Ellie, I told some of the children about movie nights on the farm and they are excited, so it's important we follow through." Ellie agreed. As long as the spirit children stayed on the farm until they decide to move on to heaven permanently, she would ensure that their stay there would be enjoyable and bear no resemblance to the past.

Ellie had been awake since five that morning. Lauren came into the bathroom after she heard the shower turn off and told her mother, "We have visitors this morning when you are ready, we will talk in the master bedroom. " Ellie quickly threw on her robe and entered the room. "Are they here yet?" Lauren nodded. Who's here?"

"Dad and Mathews." Jack proceeded to give a recap of what took place the day before and also told them, "There are other runners staying on the outskirts of the property and it frightened the children."

Mathews spoke up and said, "There is a runner that would like to come and speak with you if you are willing." Ellie was interested to hear what his part was in all the ills that had taken place there.

"Yes bring him through."

The runner spirit was there. Ellie began with her questioning "What is your name?"

Lauren translated, "Carter. I am forty years old. I was a runner, and I kidnapped girls from their families and brought them here. I never raped them, but if they let me, I would have sex with them."

Ellie wasn't buying any of his shit. "The children didn't have the right to say no because if they did you would kill them, correct?"

"Yes."

Ellie was trying to keep her anger down, because she needed to collect as much information as possible from him to help complete the story of events out there. Carter continued, "I didn't murder any children, but if I saw they were suffering I would help ease their pain quicker."

Ellie was fuming now. "So you murdered them!"

Carter then tried to justify why he had done those acts against the innocent "I had small sons and my family was starving and I needed a job."

Ellie continued with her interrogation "Would you want someone to hurt your sons and do those awful things to them?"

Carter of course replied no.

"How many children do you think lost their lives out here?"

Carter knew the answer. "Between four to five hundred." Ellie was sure the number was higher if the business had operated for forty years, given the brutality of the owners.

"What do you know about the secret society?" The runner knew nothing except those were the buyers that kept coming for the girls.

After much research, Ellie kept coming back to a secret organization a lot of businessmen belonged to and that was founded in the state around 1814. The men had to be offered a pledgeship to join by other members of like mind in order to ensure they could keep their secrets safe, no matter how dark.

They were referred to as The Masters

Ellie picked back up on her questioning of Carter. "So if you are still here, then were you murdered?"

Carter replied, "I have been staying on the outskirts of the property, and yes, I was murdered."

"What did they do to you?" Carter explained. "I wouldn't rape the really small girls, so they killed me. They cut off my legs, arms, penis, and tongue."

Ellie couldn't help but feel for anyone that crossed the owners or their policies. "I am sorry that happened to you, but if you live by the sword, you die by the sword."

He agreed. Carter said he was stuck there and couldn't move on. "I asked for forgiveness…"

Ellie had heard enough and had a final message to the runner. "You tell all the runners out there you come across that they are not welcome, and I assure you that they all will be dealt with…" He was gone.

Mathews and Jack were still after he left, so Ellie said she was sorry, but she had no patience for someone that had chosen a job that could do that to people, even if his family was starving. They both agreed.

The last runner that Jack and Mathews came across, they were able to report to the Congress, which is God's acting authoritative governing body over spirits. After all, there is a lot to keep track of. Tens of thousands of people die daily in the world. The runners that had met their own fate there at the farm were given so much time on Earth before they had to report to a much less desirable eternity. There were a few that had slipped through the cracks, so Jack and Mathews were more than willing to report them to ensure the peaceful sanctuary for those sweet souls that were still residing on the farm with the Westons.

Jack made an appearance the next evening with a woman spirit. Her name was Rachelle. Her daughter Helena, age nine, had gone missing from their yard when she was playing outside by herself. When she realized her daughter wasn't answering her yells, she left her son inside the house, as her husband was away from home at his job. She jumped on a horse and rode the path for an hour and then she passed by the farm. She saw the owners there at the property and asked if they had seen her daughter, and they said no and were acting strange. As she started to ride off, she heard her daughter's cries. Rachelle caught sight of a man walking out of a shack pulling up his trousers, and her daughter came running out behind him towards her mother.

Rachelle immediately dismounted her horse and ran towards her daughter but was shot and killed. She hasn't seen her daughter since. She was hoping to see her on the farm, but it has been so long ago she doesn't know if she is there. So many victims met such a tragic ending there on the farm that they keep themselves concealed from other spirits out of fear. Jack and Mathews were constantly meeting new spirits as news traveled in spirit world that they were there to help, which encouraged others to unveil themselves and come forward.

Rachelle left the visit after she told her story.

Jack came back a couple of hours later that evening to say that he felt weird and felt like his body was being pulled...He was nervous. Lauren told Ellie she was also getting some weird vibes that were making her feel ill, so she went on to bed. She had decided to sleep in the master bedroom since Leo was sick with the flu and needed rest, and she would be jumping in and out of bed during the night tending to the twins. Jack followed her upstairs and situated himself in the leather armchair in the master bedroom. He wasn't sure what was going to happen.

In the middle of the night Lauren had a dream she was on fire and burning, Jack woke her up and said she was covered in flames. Lauren was creeped out by what happened and didn't get much sleep the rest of the night...Things were getting weird.

The next morning when Lauren saw her mother downstairs, she told her about the long night and the awful dream she had that felt so real. Ellie took it all in. "Lauren, try not to worry about the dream. I think it was an evil spirit trying to scare you and get to you mentally."

Lauren went on to tell her mother, "Dad is feeling better and he is going to try to find out why he felt like he was being pulled away and let us know." Ellie was hoping Jack could get to the bottom of things. She didn't want to lose contact with him.

Everyone got on with the morning and starting of a new day. Ellie did her time at work and couldn't wait to get back home to everyone, especially Jack. She needed to know what was going on in spirit world. While Ellie and Lauren were bathing the girls, Jack made a quick appearance to tell them that he found out why he felt like he was being pulled. " I spoke with some other spirits on the farm, and they said I was trying to be pulled to heaven. Ellie was thankful that she had prayed hard the night before, "Please let Jack stay here with us and help the other spirits here too." She understood God was listening to her prayers.

Jack said he would be back later that night. He and Mathews came across a spirit that helped organize the raid on the farm that brought the evil to an end. Ellie was so looking forward to hearing the details of how that went down and amazed yet again at how everyone was still pulling together on both sides of life.

A couple of hours later, after the girls were fast asleep, Jack and Mathews brought forward one of the raiders. Ellie started with her acknowledgement. "Hello, what is your name?"

Lauren began to translate, "My name is Murphy, and I helped organize the raid when one of my friend's daughter went missing. Everyone started talking in the community and started hearing other families' stories about their children going missing. I lived up the road a mile for seven years and watched a lot of traffic go by on the second Monday of every month, and I felt they were up to no good. The owners of the farm gave different information throughout the years about the children and the shacks on the property. They would tell some folks they were running an orphanage, it was a children's camp, or that they were teaching children how to work on a farm." Murphy continued his story. "We caught wind they were selling children for sex, so we sent a couple of guys in to collect information and see how it all worked the next time they had a sale. They slipped in with the procession of wagons under the pretense that they were notified about the sale and there to buy girls. They watched the terrible events of the day and had all the information they needed. The next month came and the night before the sale we raided the farm at dark.

It lasted three long hours. It was chaotic, and half the men in the raid lost their lives, as well as twenty children. When the runners realized what was happening, they grabbed children out of the shacks and used them for shields.

"One of the workers rode up to the ridge to the owner's cabin and told them what was going on, so they rode down through the woods, and when they came into sight, the raiders grabbed them and strung them up and hanged them. In all there were ten adult runners that were killed that night, and the other ten runners were just children and victims themselves, so they were spared. The rest of the night was spent tearing down the shacks and burning them and cleaning up the property. All weapons were removed and everything else got thrown in the ravine. All the bodies were put into a buggy and taken off the farm to be buried, including the owners."

Ellie thought about how brave all those were that took part in the raid to rid the farm of all the evils but also couldn't believe it took forty years for the owners to get caught. She had more questions. "Murphy, how many children survived that night and what happened to them?" "There were about forty children that made it. I took nine little girls home with me and raised them like my own. We didn't have much, but they were loved and taken care of. The runner boys were taken home by some that helped in the raid. Some were reunited with their parents, and the children that were sold to the organization didn't want to go back to parents that put them in that terrible place."

Murphy told Lauren, "If you will let me, I can enter your dream and show you what the raid looked like."

Lauren agreed, and Ellie was in awe that that could be done and wished she could bear witness to that harrowing night. Ellie was a little confused. "You are here on the farm so did you die here?

"No, I passed when I was sixty-seven years old, which was an old age back then. I was forty-two when the raid happened. I just have been here staying with the children spirits."

Murphy said it was time for him to go, and Jack and Mathews followed behind him.

Lauren was a little nervous letting someone take over her dream, but she was also curious. "Mom, I am tired so I'm going to bed, and I will let you know in the morning if it worked. Good night and I love you".

"I love you too, Lauren," and they were off to bed.

The morning's noise brought Lauren down to the family room, and she told Ellie that it was the most vivid horrible dream she had ever had. Ellie had to ask, "Did you see them hanging the owners?"

"No, he kept that out of my sight, but I got a good look at the owners before that happened. She had dark brown hair and the greenest eyes I have ever seen, and he was tall, had brown hair, and really high check bones."

Ellie was trying to wrap her brain around everything. Lauren said she was really worn out and needed to lay on the couch for a few minutes before getting ready for work. Ellie told her daughter to take as much time as she needed. Alexa was entertained with cartoons, and the twins were still sleeping.

The evening brought a new visitor. Jack and Mathews came through and said they had a woman that would like to tell her story and that she had died the night of the raid. Ellie said, "Yes, please bring her through." She was there a couple of minutes later.

Lauren began, "Her name is Tally. She was twenty-six years old when she was kidnapped from her home. It took two hours by horseback to get to the farm. She was forced to be a "nurse" and survived here for five years. She was shot and killed during the raid.

The raiders didn't realize she was a victim herself and accidently shot her. They thought she was a worker for the owners."

Ellie of course had questions for her. "How many children were sold a month and how many died a month?

Tally answered, "Usually fifty to sixty children were sold a month and on average fifteen perished there a month, not including the ones that died during travel."

Ellie quickly did the math in her head based on forty years of business, "Oh my God, that means roughly twenty-eight thousand children were sold for sex and over five thousand died, not including adults and parents here on the farm . . . so heart breaking."

Ellie addressed Tally, "We are so sorry for what happened to you and we thank you for coming and telling us your story." She was gone.

Jack and Mathews said their goodbyes...They were gone.

Ellie was still sitting there at the kitchen island after the room emptied, just feeling so lost. Jack had only been gone for four months and that was unbearable as it was, but dealing with all the victims of the child sex trafficking operation was almost as hard. She was still trying to grasp what all had happened there on their farm; such cruelty had found so many.

Chapter Five
Truth Shall Set You Free

The planned trip that Lauren and Ellie were looking forward to was finally here. They had both decided on Vegas since neither had ever been and it was on both of their bucket lists. The girls were going to Leo's mother's house for the weekend, and the dogs were being looked after by Chance, even though he was not thrilled about it. Everything was ready for their departure the next day, and they were excited to get away for a mother-daughter outing and to do a little shopping, even if they were only going to be gone for two days.

When they arrived at their hotel, they were an hour early for their check-in, so they slipped into the bar/restaurant and ordered an appetizer and the best Bloody Mary they had ever had. It was topped with a large shrimp tail and a piece of crisp bacon. Once their bags were deposited in their room, they headed to the strip a couple of blocks away and to Caesars Palace for a little gambling and designer handbag shopping.

They finished up their day at a bar in Caesars with a fruity frozen drink and reflected on what all they had seen and the Louis Vuitton handbag that Lauren had always wanted and finally splurged on. Ellie was smiling at Lauren while she was admiring her new bag. "Your dad would be happy for you that you finally bought one since you've wanted a Louis since you were eight." They both giggled. "Yes, I think he would be proud of me, "Lauren said, followed by more laughter.

The next day was more of the same—shopping, a little gambling, and drinks—after all, they were in Vegas. By that evening, both Lauren and Ellie had enjoyed their little outing but were looking forward to jumping on the plane the next morning to get back home to the farm, those sweet little girls, and Jack. It was nice to escape their reality for a brief moment, but they had so much work to do and so many people counting on them.

When they arrived home the next afternoon and walked into the farmhouse, Jack was waiting for them. Lauren looked at Ellie and grinned, "Dad's here."

"Hello Jack, we are so glad to be home!"

"Dad says he is glad we went, but he is also glad we are home and that things were pretty quiet while we were gone."

Ellie got busy taking care of the house and dogs while Lauren went to retrieve the girls from Leo's parents—back into the fray. Another work week was underway on the living and spirit side with everyone doing what they needed to do. By mid-week things got interesting for the Westons, especially for Lauren.

Ellie was working a little late at the office on Wednesday evening when she received a call from home. It was Lauren. "Hi sweetie, what's up?"

Lauren acted cool but she felt the need to call her mother. "Earlier when I was upstairs, I smelled an awful burnt smell, and now I smell it downstairs."

Ellie's first thought was that Lauren left something on. "Did you leave your hair straightener on?"

"No Mom, nothing is on. Ellie then remembered what Jack had told them during one of his first visits: If you smell a foul burnt smell, that is a very evil spirit. Do not anger them.

"Lauren, do you want me to come home right now?"

"No, I am fine, just curious when you would be home. . . ."

Ellie knew she needed to wrap things up and get to the farm. "I am shutting down my computer and heading that way."

Lauren seemed to be relieved to hear her mother would be there in ten minutes or so. Leo was working nights for the next two weeks on a construction site, and she was there alone with the girls. When Ellie pulled up to the house, Lauren walked out, and Ellie jumped out of her vehicle.

"Where are the girls?

"Down for a nap. Dad is here. You are never going to believe who wants to come speak with us . . . Mary Ellen!"

Lauren continued, "Dad said that was who I was smelling, and he and Mathews ran into her here in the house."

Ellie was mystified. "Why in the hell isn't she in Hell?"

"Dad said he doesn't know all the answers but will see what he can find out. He said that she wants to speak with us."

Ellie started to rant. "Oh I have plenty to say to that woman. Are you up for it Lauren?"

"I think so. Dad said he could bring her through this evening."

"That's fine by me." Ellie thought, poor Mathews has to see that woman who watched him being burned alive and did nothing. Teddy, Mathews father—or so he thought—had confessed to him when they made contact that he was not his father, but that Thomas was, the very man that murdered Mathews and Teddy.

Mathews wasn't around for a few days, and Ellie just assumed he was making up for lost time with Teddy, but he was devasted by all that had been disclosed to him by the only father he had ever known. Mathews kept to himself to digest what had been revealed to him. Once Teddy confessed the truth, he left for heaven permanently without letting Mathews know his plan, which made Mathews feel twice the loss.

Jack finally told Lauren and Ellie because they kept noticing he was showing up without his best friend and they kept pressing him for answers. Mathews started coming back around, and Ellie told him not to worry and reassured him that the Westons loved him and that he was a part of their family, no matter who his parents were.

Before Jack left the visit, he said it would be late when they brought Mary Ellen through, and Ellie agreed to it. All the girls finally got to sleep, and around midnight Lauren came downstairs with a twin in her arms and said, "They are here, but I need to change a diaper really quick upstairs and then I will be back down."

Ellie was exhausted so she laid back down on the couch and waited. When Lauren came back down, she relayed what Jack had told her. "Well I guess she didn't want to wait and took off. Dad said they are going to try and find her."

Ellie commented, "I guess her time is more important." Jack told them that after she had a conversation with Lauren and Ellie she had to report back to Hell.

"Why was she allowed to leave in the first place?" Ellie questioned, yet another answer Jack would have to get.

•   •   •

The morning came with its busy routine: Leo rolling in from the night shift, dogs needing to be attended to, and all the other chores that got done before the babies were awakened to start the day. Ellie had just walked back in the door from walking the two little inside dogs, and Lauren announced, "Dad and Mathews are here with her."

Ellie quickly responded. "I'm ready" and took a seat at the kitchen island.

Lauren said, "Okay, she's come through now."

Ellie looked at Lauren and asked, "Is that her?"

Lauren turned and looked in another direction, then back at her mother. "Yes that's her." Ellie knew that Mary Ellen had been revealed to Lauren in the dream about the raid and could positively identify her.

Ellie's next question was her standard to all that came through. "What is your name?"

Lauren vocalized her response. "You know what my name is!"

Ellie knew she just wanted her to answer. "Your name is Mary Ellen."

She responded yes.

Ellie continued. "What is your last name?"

Mary Ellen refused to tell them, so Ellie assured her that she would figure that out as well as dig up every horrific piece of information she could on her and her husband.

Mary Ellen then quickly tried to defend her actions. "None of you could have survived my life and what all I had to do." Ellie assured her none of them would ever have wanted her life and they would have gladly protected those children. She went on to tell Mary Ellen that if she was truly a victim herself she could have killed her husband Thomas in his sleep and ended the brutal raping and killing of those children, but she chose not to because money was too important to her.

Mary Ellen was becoming irritated that her last Hail Mary attempt for redemption and forgiveness would not be found there in the Weston's home, and she popped off "Well I guess I will just head back to Hell."

Ellie said, "Wait a minute, why did you come in the first place?"

"Because you were allowing others to come through for visits and to talk."

Ellie was disturbed by her reply. "Yes we have been speaking with your victims!"

Mary Ellen realized that God had made his judgement long ago, but Ellie was the judge and jury today, and her judgement was the same condemnation—Mary Ellen needed to stay in the dark murky pool of Hell where she belonged.

Lauren spoke up. "She's gone."

Ellie immediately started addressing everyone left in the room even though she couldn't see two thirds of them. "Did that woman really just try to justify all the evils she did? She better stay in Hell or I am personally going to drag her by her hair to the gates myself, whether it is in this life or the next."

Ellie then asked Jack, "How was she able to leave anyway?"

Jack wasn't sure how she had negotiated that deal, but he did assure his family that she would never be coming back. Ellie was relieved to hear that; they had enough going on without having to deal with that shit.

Alexa was still asleep on the couch and just starting to stir when Jack said, "I love you both so much and I will see you later this evening."

Lauren said, "Dad's gone." It was time to get ready and head out the door for another workday, despite everyone not wanting to.

•   •   •

The next couple of days were uneventful, then things started to get weird again. Jack seemed completely down in the dumps, and Mathews hadn't been by with him lately and had stayed away for the rest of the week. When Jack came through towards the end of the week, Ellie started pressing him about what was going on and why he and Mathews were so down in the dumps.

Jack knew he couldn't and shouldn't keep anything from Ellie, so he told them what they had just discovered, and Lauren repeated the disturbing news. "Dad said that they have met other spirits that died back on the Bennington property. They were used for experiments and kept in two or three shacks that were guarded. "

Ellie quickly started asking what all happened back there, and Lauren kept repeating her father's news. "They would do things like cut off peoples arms and legs and try to reattach them to other people. They would see how fast people would bleed out with certain injuries. They would make people eat vegetation so they would know what was poisonous and what wasn't, and they would also inject people with chemicals to see what would happen to them."

Jack told them that these acts were performed by "Doc," according to the spirits, but even the children spirits realized they were monsters, no matter what they called themselves. The next week brought new visitors with new information:

- Gage, age forty-four: There was a big depression in 1837 and he was homeless, so the owners said he could stay in the back in one of their shacks, but as soon as he got to the farm he was quickly used for human experimentation. He lasted ten years back there. They first started injecting him with chemicals, and they kept him sedated by feeding him poppies. They eventually cut off one of his legs and tried to attach someone else's leg, but he got an infection and died.

- Lela, age seventeen: She was kidnapped from her home and used for experiments at the back of the farm. They impregnated her and fed her a bunch of food and injected her with chemicals. When the baby was born, her bones were so brittle and the baby was so big that her pelvis broke and her vertebrae was crushed, leaving her paralyzed. The baby wasn't named, and they quickly started to inject him with chemicals, making him have seizures, and he died. Her legs became infected, and she died.

- Judson, age nineteen: He was kidnapped and forced to have sex with Lela so she would become pregnant. It took months because they would set her on top of him and nothing would happen, but they eventually became friends and she became pregnant. Once they realized she was in fact pregnant, Judson was of no use to them anymore, so they killed him. (They remain together still on the farm.)

- Tad, age thirty: He was kidnapped. It was an hour horse-ride to the farm. He had a limp, so they cut off his leg at the hip and he bled to death.

- Brittney, age eight: Very smart! She was used for experiments. They tried to extract bone marrow, and she developed an infection and died from it. She lasted about a year there.

- Girl, age seven: She was born there in a shack and wasn't given a name. She never felt the sun on her skin; she was kept locked in the shack, and they did experiments on her. Girl died the night of the raid, she thinks, from smoke inhalation. The raiders didn't realize there were victims and an overseer in the shacks and they burned them down.

- Garrett, age thirteen: Kidnapped while walking a not heavily traveled horse path. Two men approached him claiming to be doctors and said they could help him; he was blind in his left eye, and he was starting to turn yellow—he was jaundiced. He agreed to go with them. It was about an hour walk, and when they arrived at the farm and went to the back, they immediately strapped him down and poked his legs about a hundred times to collect blood samples. He cried for several days begging them to let him return home to his parents; he knew his health was not good. They refused, and he died a few days later.

- Jaden, age fifteen: She was kidnapped, and she didn't sell at auction so after a few sales they moved her to the back in a shack, and the last thing she remembers is falling asleep and she never woke back up.

- Frederick, age thirty: Killed in 1837. Thomas confided in him and told him how he made his money and took him to the farm to show him. When Thomas rode to the back of the property, Frederick waited at the front and a twenty-six-year-old woman asked Frederick to help her escape and told him all the evils that took place there. They had just made it to the horse path when Thomas rode up and asked him if he paid for the girl, and he replied no. Thomas shot him.

- Kip, age eighteen: Was kidnapped. It took a month travel to get to the farm. They tried to make him a runner after a week of being there and he refused, so they hanged him.

- Johnson, age forty-two: Helped with the raid. His brother Garrison was friends with the owners, and he also was in the raid party. Both perished that night.

- ? age thirties: He didn't want to give his name or exact age. He helped organize the raid. He said one had been planned earlier and some of the participants became nervous and backed out because they knew some would die, but a short time later, they revised their plan and executed it. He said the owners tried to be friends with everyone but not get too close with anyone to help deflect suspicion about their operation.

- Jolé, age twenty-three: Came from France and had an accent. She was kidnapped, and it took over a month to arrive at the farm. She was their first amputee. They cut her leg off below the knee, and she made it a year. She thinks she died of poisoning.

- Cam, age thirty: Was kidnapped and forced to work as "Doc's" assistant. He was forced to give injections, and when "Doc" wanted him to cut off someone's leg, he refused, and they shot him. He said "Doc" had a very thick accent and thought he might have come from England; Cam overheard a conversation that the United States was trying to catch up with Europe's much-advanced medicine/medical knowledge.

- Jeget, age thirty: Was forced to work as "Doc's" assistant. He was forced to give injections. He had a boat hiding, and he was waiting for his chance to escape…They caught on, and they killed him.

- Silas, age twenty-three: First gay man in the county. He rolled cigarettes for a living, as he did not want to work on his parent's farm. They loved and supported their son knowing he was gay. When

Thomas heard about Silas, he sought him out and approached him with the idea that he could help find a partner for him, and Silas was excited at the thought of finding a soul mate and partner for life so he went with Thomas to the farm. When he first got there, they treated him very well, gave him a shack in the back, and clothed him and fed him well. He rolled cigarettes in return and made pretty little dresses for the girls. Silas soon learned why he was asked to make the dresses for the girls to be sold.

He said Thomas wore the finest of clothes and always had sunglasses on

He was forced to physically be with a straight young man named Jasper who was twenty. Jasper had bad acne, and he was approached by someone who said they could help him get rid of it, so he gladly went with them to the farm.

He quickly realized they were bad people and up to no good. They cut off his pretty long hair and then started injecting him with chemicals until Silas came along. They would force Silas to penetrate Jasper and then study the effects, sometimes making them do it several times a day. Jasper wasn't gay, but he developed feelings for Silas, as he was kind and gentle to him. Silas was also forced to have sex with animals.

Silas was allowed to write to his parents, and one day Silas wrote them a letter stating they were doing terrible things to him and using him for experiments, and he begged them to come get him. Someone intercepted the letter and read it. They hung Silas and made Jasper watch. Jasper died a short time later, he thinks from a broken heart. Even though he was a straight man, they were all each other had.

They became friends and are still friends now and together on the farm.

- Kat thirty-nine and Robert forty-two, married: They were Thomas and Mary Ellen's neighbors about three miles up the road. They became suspicious of their activities because they noticed a lot of traffic and strangers,dressed in black going to Thomas' house. They decided to follow Thomas one day, and they arrived at the farm. Thomas rode through to the back, and Kat and Robert watched from the horse path. A runner approached them and asked if they were there to purchase a girl. They understood the rottenness of their business and politely said no as Thomas was approaching. They turned to leave, and Thomas asked the runner what he had said to them, and the runner repeated what he had asked them. Thomas shot him and then turned the gun on Kat and Robert and shot and killed them. The year was 1833.

- Bearded Man, age fifties: He was too nervous to give his name, said he was killed there on the farm before the raid, and he was not a friend of Thomas's. He said the owners were smart, that they kept fake ledgers, and that if you dig in the ravine you will find coins, jewelry, and bones. He said the Westons were playing with fire when it came to Thomas. He was leaving for heaven, where it was safe, immediately after the visit,. He didn't know if Thomas was in communication with his living family.

- Nancy, age sixty-seven: Her husband had passed away, and they had no children. All their bills were paid. There was no debt against the property, but one day someone showed up and forced her off the property. They knew she had no family and no one to turn to for help, as the land was still very much lawless. She survived two winters out in the elements with just a blanket and traveled the backwoods in the township and was staying in the woods on the farm in hiding, drinking spring water and eating water cress at night to survive. One day she was spotted by runners as they were disposing of bodies in the ravine, so they killed her.

- Tom, age fifty-six: He lived two-days travel from Stenson and was in town visiting family and friends. While he was eating at the local tavern, he noticed a posting on the wall. The post read "For a good time" and gave directions to the farm, so he decided since he wasn't married and that it was an option, he ventured out there. Once he arrived, they brought out three girls between the ages of eight and nine to choose from, and he informed them that that was not his idea of a good time, and he turned around to leave in disgust, so they shot him in the back and killed him.

- Patricia, age forty-two: Mary Ellen's best friend. She said Mary Ellen had a drug problem and tics because of it. When she would visit their home there would be lots of money laying around. Their house was two or three miles from the farm, but Mary Ellen and Thomas didn't live together. Patricia told others what they were up to, and it got back to Thomas, so they lured her to the farm and killed her. (She confirmed that Mary Ellen and Thomas were Matthew's biological parents.)

- Blaine, age twenty-eight: She was Thomas' girlfriend and stayed with him at the cabin in the back of property. She said they were in love. His wife Mary Ellen lived at another location and would only stay at the cabin the night before an auction. Blaine became pregnant with Thomas' child, so when she went into labor it lasted a long time, and Thomas left the cabin for more linens, his wife Mary Ellen walked in right when the baby was born. She was able to hold her baby boy for just a few moments after she gave birth. Then Mary Ellen killed her before Thomas could return. (Mary Ellen and Thomas named the baby Benton.)

- Adam, age twelve: He was kidnapped and used in the back for experiments. He was forced to let older men take him, and his anus and colon developed tears that became infected, and he wound up with an infection throughout his whole body and developed a fever of 105 degrees. He said it felt like his eyes were bleeding. They put him in a metal tub with cold water from the spring, but he died a short time later.

- Matson, age twenty: He was a gay young man. He was kidnapped from a farm field he was working on, and it took four to five days travel by horse to get to the farm, from where he was taken They first tried to sell him as a gay young man, but no one wanted to buy him; they wanted the little boys. So after a few auctions they moved him to the back of the property to do experiments. They made him have sex with other men and animals, and then they started injecting his penis with infections, and they bred him with a female to see how it would affect the baby because sexually transmitted diseases were almost nonexistent then. She gave birth to a baby girl, and the baby's head wasn't formed right, and her legs were turned out. They let Matson and the girl care for the baby until their baby passed away sixty days later. After that he was ready to die. He had been stuck there for seven years, and he had had everything taken away from him. The last experiment they did to him was to cut off his penis and attach a horse penis to him. "Doc" didn't want to do it, but Thomas held a gun over him. He told Matson he would make it so he couldn't feel anything. He died a short time later. (He said "Doc" would document all procedures/experiments and keep daily notes.)

Ellie and Lauren now understood why Jack and Mathews found a new level of sorrow after hearing those horrible stories of victims being used as scientific experiments against their will, with the outcome always being death. After receiving those visitors, a robin appeared and kept crashing into the patio door in the master bedroom upstairs and leaving a white film that covered the glass, and that had gone on for several days. When a couple of spirits came through for a visit after the robin started its annoying attack on the door, they mentioned the robin and said it was possessed and that Ellie needed to kill it.

One morning that week, Jack was visiting with his family when he was suddenly summoned for a special meeting, so he said his goodbye and said he would be back to see them. Ellie turned to Lauren. "I wonder what that was all about?" Lauren said she wasn't sure but that he would be back later, so Ellie finished up a couple of chores, and out the door she went to start her work day. Ellie hadn't been at her desk longer than ten minutes when Lauren phoned her and said, "Dad is here and says Thomas wants to talk."

Ellie was stunned yet again. "I thought He was in Hell with no way out?"

Lauren responded, "Yeah, I don't know, Dad is working on answers." Ellie said she would be right there and she closed out the documents she was working on and flew home.

When she walked into the house and made it into the kitchen, Lauren said, "You need to sit down."

Ellie replied, "I don't want to sit down. Is he here?"

"He is getting ready to come through, but you need to sit down." Ellie was already irritated with this meeting, but she reluctantly took a seat in the rocking chair in the family room. Lauren said, "He's here."

Ellie asked, "Is that him?" Lauren glanced his way, then back at Ellie, and she gave a nod, then Thomas started to speak through Lauren.

"You know that annoying robin hitting your door upstairs? That is my doing. I find you speaking with the other spirits and digging in the ravine just as annoying, so if you don't stop something might happen to your daughter or grandchildren. Are you ready to make a deal with the devil?"

Ellie was quiet for a moment. She wasn't sure what kind of powers he did have, but she was not going to be bullied or threatened by the likes of him or Satan. "You pathetic shit! We don't need to speak with anymore spirits to understand how many people you raped and murdered, but if they want to keep talking, we will keep listening and taking notes. What's your last name Thomas? Edwards? Dolby? Nowling? You have used all those names on documents and when introducing yourself."

Ellie had been researching and was starting to unravel the truth about Thomas and his horrible wife, and she had no intentions of stopping. The rain had continued for three months, and they hadn't been able to bring in heavy equipment to dig, so she had been going home after work in the evenings and on the weekends and digging in the ravine herself. She was amazed at what all she found so far: hundreds of old medicine bottles, medical devices, pieces of leather coats worn by the runners, leather straps with chains attached, and even an old pair of Thomas' sunglasses. During one of her digs Ellie also found a small rib and clavicle still intact, a child's femur, and a girl's soft leather shoe

That was the hardest find, as she fought back tears. It was one thing to speak about what would be found in that ravine, but it was another to pull the items out with her own hands and imagine the terrible suffering some of the victims went through and how terrifying those moments had to have been.

Thomas started back in. "I have living family that are very wealthy and powerful that I need to protect. This is your last chance to agree to stop, or I am coming after your family." Ellie just smiled and told Thomas the meeting was over, so Jack, Mathews, and Thomas left the meeting. Lauren asked if her mother would wait until she got the girls up and dressed so they could leave at the same time because she had creepy vibes. Her mother understood and agreed. Alexa was still fast asleep on the couch in the family room, and Lauren ran upstairs to get the twins out of their cribs.

While Ellie waited downstairs, she ran the conversation with Thomas through her head. She had no doubt he probably could be menacing, but she thought a lot of it was smoke and mirror tactics. Lauren rounded the corner with a twin dangling in each arm and handed one of them to her mother to change, and in the middle of putting on a new diaper on her squirming grandchild, her daughter said something and Ellie didn't quite catch it, so she looked up, and her daughter said, "Go ahead and finish that."

The hair on the back of her neck stood up. It was her daughter's voice, but it was not her tone, nor was the smirk, so Ellie quickly got the diaper fastened and the twin crawled away on the floor. She looked her daughter in the eyes, and he started his threats. "You know I could make her have a fatal seizure, or she could have an accident carrying the twins down the stairs." Then he manipulated Lauren's head with a quick jerk to one side to emphasize his warnings. Ellie kept calm and grabbed Lauren's hands and started rubbing them and her face, telling her she loved her. Thomas spoke up. "That's not going to work." But Ellie just ignored what was coming out of her daughter's mouth and told her God was with them. That seemed to bring her back and make Thomas bug out.

Lauren was still sitting on the overstuffed chair and her mother was still rubbing her daughter's hands when Lauren glanced down and grinned and asked her mother, "What are you doing?" Ellie went on to explain that Thomas had possessed her. As Jack was coming through in a panic, he said that Thomas slipped back into the house and put up a perimeter forcefield around the Weston's house so that Jack and Mathews weren't able to enter. Ellie didn't know which was more alarming: the possession or the forcefield.

Jack told them to hurry and leave the house and that he and Mathews would try to get answers to why Thomas was allowed out of Hell and what could they do to protect their family. There was so much to the spirit world and a lot to know, even after two hundred years there, it seemed there were still so many unknowns for those that chose to stay.

Ellie made it home early that evening to find Lauren and the girls all settled into their day's end routine and Leo working next door on their house. "Is your dad here, Lauren?"

"Yes, he's here. He said that they were able to put up a protective forcefield around the property but doesn't know how long that will last. He also said to ignore the robin and that it will die in a couple of days. "Ellie felt a little more at ease to hear that news but knew that they would be dealing with Thomas in the future.

The next four days brought new spirits and new stories from those that knew Thomas and Mary Ellen:

- Thomas rode into a small town about ten miles north of Stenson, now known as Jessup, that consisted of eight or nine houses. He showed up with armed runners and told the families that had assembled that one person from every household had to volunteer to go with him. Henry Sr. volunteered from his clan, as he was sixty years old and life expectancy wasn't much past that at the time. Most that were sent were young children. The next oldest was a fourteen-year-old boy. They weren't sure why they were being forced to go though. Maybe there was a war going on somewhere and they needed help.

When they arrived at the farm they were taken to the back, where the experiment shacks were, and they informed the fourteen-year-old boy they were going to castrate him, so Henry Sr. stood up to object, and they shot him. He does not know what happened to the others after he died, but when the visit was over, he was moving on to heaven to look for his family.

- Garrett age thirty-five: He was an inventor and created farming methods. He was a friend of Thomas' and they met on the town square in Stenson every two weeks on Wednesdays. One day Thomas invited him out to the farm to show him what he did for a living, and once Garrett saw the small girls and Thomas explained, he became disgusted and turned to leave when Thomas shot him in the back.

- Two couples, Betsy and Edmond and Howe and Myrtle: Lived together nine miles north of Stenson while Howe and Myrtle's house was being built. Betsy and Edmond were friends of Thomas and Mary Ellen. One day they were invited for lunch in Stenson, and Thomas encouraged them to bring Howe and Myrtle so they could be introduced to them. When they arrived back home, it was very quiet, so they went inside hollering for their children

- Betsy and Edmond had two daughters, ages eight and twelve, and a son, age fifteen. Howe and Myrtle had a son, age thirteen. The children were nowhere to be found. The parents went to the neighbors south of them and were told that they had seen a buggy full of people drive by with children in it, and as they kept traveling south, there were other witnesses that repeated the same sighting, so they worked their way to the farm and once they caught sight of one of the boys, they knew they had found them. All four of them dismounted their houses and ran onto the property. Runners emerged from the woods with a long sword-type weapon, and in one fell swoop a runner sliced both Howe and Myrtle and killed them, and as Betsy and Edmond ran toward their children, they were both shot dead in front of them. The girls were sold, and their son was forced to be a runner, and he perished the night of the raid. (The organization would not only burn bodies and throw them in a ravine, but they also tossed their victims in the river that was less than a mile from the farm.)

- Camille, age four: Jack helped her tell her story. She was considered an "elite child" of "Blood Royalty," conceived on the farm by Thomas and raised there until the raid, and the night of the raid she was killed by the "raiders." The elite children were not sold and were treated much better than the other children. They were fed good food (and not fed other children), and they were dressed better than the others, with dresses that had fancy lace, embroidery work, and glass beads sewn on them. They also wore nice brown leather shoes.

- Henry, age eleven: His father was in the "secret society" and wore a blue coat. He traded Henry to Thomas for a girl (for sexual pleasure). He lasted three months on the farm. He witnessed girls being raped, beaten, and sick and starving kids, and couldn't take it anymore so he hanged himself. Once his father received the news, he became distraught and eventually took his own life. Henry said his family life was good until his father joined the secret society.

- Patrice, age sixty-two: Patrice and her husband lived a little more than a mile up the road from the farm. They didn't have any children, and when her husband passed away, Thomas took her farm from her, allowed her to live there, and made her work on the farm. She was working there one day and she said she believes she had a stroke and died of natural causes.

- Gallett, age twenty-four: She was lost to Thomas by her husband in a card game. She lasted three years there. One day there was an auction and she couldn't stomach it anymore, so when a buggy drove by she tried to flag them down and was shot. She mentioned they kept an orphanage sign up, but the day of an auction they took it down. She also said that the sickest thing she witnessed on the farm was them feeding children other children. Some of the children grew so distraught they would try to kill themselves by eating their own feces and ingesting chemicals.

- Margie, age fourteen: She was sold to Thomas by her father. The night of the raid she was killed. A runner put a big knife in her hand, and the runners ran to the back of property (cowards), and so the raiders thought she was a worker (not a victim), and they killed her. She tended to the small crops and took care of Thomas' children; they were called the elites and they all too perished in the raid. Even though they were young children, the raiders wanted to end Thomas' blood line.

- Natalie, age thirteen: Watched her eight-year-old sister get kidnapped, and she followed them to the farm, as they lived a mile north of it. When she ran onto the property, the runners ran out of the woods and dragged her back into woods and hit her in the back of her head, killing her. She didn't know what happened to her sister.

- Bonnelle, age twenty-one: Was orphaned by her parents at age sixteen when they were accused of robbing the tavern and hanged for it. She was brought to the farm and considered a "prime piece" and was raped often. She made friends with a runner, Coop, age seventeen, and they planned to run off but were caught and shot. She said her jobs there were to boil dandelions for tea and scrape and beat cow hides.

- Lester, age thirty-seven: Lived in Stenson and was killed in 1829. He was friends with Thomas and would donate money for the orphanage; he didn't know it was a child sex trafficking operation. He had been by the farm a couple of times, but when he visited the last time, he thought something seemed off. Then he heard a girl scream and run out of the shack with blood down the front of her dress and a young man in his twenties pulling up his trousers. He then understood what kind of place it was. Thomas caught sight of him, and when he approached, Lester told him he wouldn't be donating any more money and for Thomas to give all the money back to him that he donated because he did not support that kind of place. Thomas assured him he couldn't have his money back before he shot him.

- Cleo, age fourteen: Lived a couple miles north of Jessup and was kidnapped. When she arrived at the farm, she quickly understood that she would never see her parents again, that the farm was horrifying and brutal, and that you just had to accept what was going to happen to you. She tried to escape with a friend she made and was shot and killed.

- Maureen, age eight: She was kidnapped in 1832, and it took several hours by horse to arrive at the farm. She was there a couple of months, and it was three days until the auction so all the girls had to bathe. She was the last one, and by then the water was black. They gave her a very hard sponge to bathe with and she cut her skin with it. She died three days later from an infection.

- Alice, age thirteen: She was kidnapped from Springfield, Illinois. She was auctioned and sold, and as she was leaving the platform she tripped and fell and broke her neck when her head landed on a step.

- Augusta, age fourteen: Kidnapped from her farm just the next county over in 1843. She was there on the farm for two years before she was sold at auction. A man wearing a black coat purchased her and then dragged her into a shack, raped and strangled her.

- Christian, age eleven: Kidnapped and brought to the farm to be a runner two days before the raid. He was killed the night of the raid by raiders; they stabbed him and it was a terrible death that took thirty agonizing minutes before he passed. (The raid happened in 1854.)

- Clementine, age sixteen: She was kidnapped from an adjoining county, and it took several hours by horse to arrive at the farm. She was there for two months and was raped ("broke in) and was killed the night of the raid.

- Frances, age twenty: Kidnapped in 1834 and died in 1846. He was kidnapped out of his yard, and his mother was strangled in front of him by a runner. He was eight years old. He started out in front of the farm with them trying to make him a runner and then they moved him to the back. They did all kinds of experiments on him and finally started injecting him with red, green, and white milky substances... He died of organ failure.

- Glynn, age thirty-two: Her daughter was kidnapped from their farm field while working. Glynn had heard about the orphanage in the next county over, so she rode a few hours to the farm to look for Holly but when she arrived was captured and forced to be a slave. She was forced to eat the runners' scraps, and if they consumed too much alcohol and vomited up their food, that was her dinner. There was a runner that became infatuated with her, and when she refused to marry him, they put her head on a log and decapitated her. Glynn's daughter sold at auction, and she doesn't know what became of her.

- Tanessa, age sixteen: Was kidnapped while walking along a horse path to join her father fishing the river; they lived two counties from the farm. She was at the farm for a week and developed an infection that turned her fingers and toes black (it was mid-summer). She died a few days later.

Lauren and Ellie knew the majority of the spirits left for heaven immediately after being freed from that terrible place, but so many chose to stay and develop friendships with those that suffered just as much, and now they were befriending the Westons and becoming a part of their family. All their stories were sad and unimaginable, but they all kept giving Lauren and Ellie the same advice…Be happy

The Westons were happy. They were trying to be happy but had been through so much, and now meeting and listening to those that lost everything made them want to let the little things go and handle their spiritual business inside their home with no fear. Ellie had cleaned the glass door enough and was tired of the robin smashing into it, so she instructed Leo to shoot it with a pellet gun and be done with it. She did not like the idea of harming any animal, but there was nothing more to do for that bird than to put it out of its misery. Its brain was forever scrambled by Thomas. The next day at dawn Leo took care of the robin and then buried it.

After several days of the latest spirits coming through to tell all they knew about the terrible owners some of them called friends, Thomas made another unexpected visit. They had just finished up a visit with Patrice telling them how Thomas stole her farm when Jack said there was a surprise visitor coming through, and before Ellie could ask who was it, Lauren said "Thomas is here."

Ellie hated hearing those words and wasn't sure quite what to expect, but Thomas immediately started talking. "I don't care if you continue to dig in the ravine and speak with the other spirits, but you can't go public with any information because my family is powerful and rich and I need to protect them. Ellie could tell by Lauren's translation of Thomas's words that he understood that they were not going to be intimidated by him and that his approach was much different with them that night, but Ellie had had enough.

It was her turn to speak. "I am not making any deals with you, and we will be going public with the horrible truths about what you and Mary Ellen did out here on the farm and everywhere else your path of brutality went." Ellie was disgusted by his complete ignorance and conceitedness regarding the concern of tarnishing his and his family's name while giving no thought to all the small children that were taken from their families and were raped, murdered, and sold—not to mention the killing of his own children…All for what? Money?

Ellie continued her blasting of him and his lack of a moral compass. "You aren't smart, Thomas, like everyone has been telling us. You are just conniving! If you are so smart you could have made money that didn't involve the brutality and murder of so many innocent souls. By the way, I had your robin killed, so we will not be bothered by your antics anymore."

Jack spoke up and said it was time for Thomas to leave and that Mathews was personally escorting him back to Hell's perimeter, where he would be eternally locked down, not to ever return. Ellie then understood why his attitude and tone had changed. He had tried to make them fearful, but it didn't work, and what she was hearing now was him being resolved to the fact that the game was over for him. There was nothing more he could do to them or the others who chose to stay at the farm…He left the visit.

When Andrews returned just a few minutes later, Ellie was curious if Thomas had said anything to him on the escort. Andrews answered, "Well, that was awkward. No, he didn't say anything and neither did I." Ellie thanked him for his help and apologized. That had to have been hard, after all, it was his own father.

The Westons continued on their now daily norm of life with work, finishing Lauren's house, digging the ravine, and speaking with the spirits. In the last couple of visits, Ellie could tell someone was trying to interfere with Lauren's translations because she would keep her eyes closed like she was drifting off to sleep, her words would be slurred, and the interpretations would get jumbled. Ellie finally spoke up and said, "Lauren, I'm pretty sure you are getting interference from another spirit," and Jack agreed and told them that he and Mathews would try to catch who was doing it. The spirit world was a mysterious place sometimes. With no handbook to help guide them, they had to figure things out as they were thrown at them.

Ellie thought that since Mary Ellen and Thomas had made their appearance, there was one person left: "Doc" , besides the continual pesky runners that were pushed over the property perimeter causing them to fall into their already determined, Hell, once they showed themselves. Spirits only have so much energy, just like the living, and according to Jack it drains a lot of energy to conceal themselves from other spirits, and eventually their veil would drop and they would be spotted.

It was a couple of days later when Jack and Mathews came for a visit and Jack told Ellie, "You were right. That was Doc interfering." They had finally spotted him in the house. Mathews hurried to catch up with him once he fled to see if he would come back and speak with everybody, but he just turned and said "boo" to Mathews. He said he didn't have time; he was trying to figure out why his house was flooding, and he said he had nowhere else to stay. The spirit world was closing in on him. Doc had been staying in the house he resided in back on the farm when he worked for Thomas. There were remnants still there and there was a concrete basement that he used for a lab that was full of water, as Ellie had made several trips back there in years past.

Ellie surmised that his final destination was hell and that it was catching up with him; that's why the flooding was taking place where he hung out, so that he would be pushed to his eternity. She also guessed he would come back for a visit and act like he was the victim so that the Westons would take pity on him and allow him to stay…That wasn't going to happen. He had taken so many lives when he just should have taken a bullet sooner. Sure enough, by evenings end the first visitor to make an appearance was Doc.

When Doc came through, he admitted he had been causing interference and listening to their conversations. He also told them he went to heaven a few times to look for his family, but he was not allowed back.

It was time for Ellie to find out as much as she could before he became antsy and left the visit. She first wanted to know where he came from and how he became acquainted with Thomas. Doc began: "I met Thomas in a tavern in London, England in the early 1820s. There was an auction that night for prostitutes and a bar fight broke out, and I was tending to one of the guys that had a large laceration on top of his head from a beer mug being broken over it. Thomas asked me to step outside when I was finished stitching the gentleman up, and I complied. He told me he could make me a rich doctor over in the United States, which sounded appealing to me since we weren't paid that well in London, and I thought I could go over there and send money back home to my family. "

Doc went on. "Thomas and I boarded a ship, and he brought me here to the farm. Once I arrived, I was placed in the little house in the back across the creek, and at first I was paid very well, and then the money stopped and I became a victim myself. Thomas would stand over me and tell me what to do with his hand on his gun, so I did what I was told because he also threatened me that he would board a ship back to London and kill my family, so I was forced to do those heinous experiments."

Ellie was ready to speak her mind, "You should have taken the bullet up front! Did those children and adults beg you for their lives?"

"Yes, sometimes, but I had no choice." Ellie assured him he did have a choice and that he should have taken it.

Doc asked if he could stay on the Westons farm before he left the visit, and Ellie said they would get back with him…She had no intention of agreeing to that. After Doc left, she conversed with Jack and Mathews and said some of the other spirits would be more traumatized if he were here and that she couldn't have it.

Jack assured her that Mathews was reporting him to the congress and that that should help his journey along to where he belonged. Once he was removed from the Bennington property and Jack and Mathews had confirmation on that, they received a surprise visit from Doc's wife. It was a couple of days later when she came forward, and Ellie knew it would bring more information on him.

Ellie started the visit through Lauren as she always did. "What is your name?"

She replied, "Kat." Ellie wasn't sure if that was short for Katherine, but she kept talking, and they listened. "I was going to meet my father one day. He was fishing off the pier at the New York harbor, and I saw Robert Pemberton filing down the walkway with everybody else and I caught his eye. We were married thirty days later. I was eighteen and he was twenty-seven years old."

"We traveled to Stenson, and we lived with some friends for ten years in town while he worked on the farm, where he stayed a lot of the time. We had two children. He would take a couple of trips a year to travel back to London. He would travel with a couple of colleagues, and we had to stay back. Things just seemed odd, so I finally decided to go out to the farm and surprise him. When I got there and told them who I was, one of the workers there in the front brought me back to where Robert was working."

"Robert greeted me with an odd nervousness and told me he had something for me, and he put a blind fold on me. I was thinking he had a nice surprise, but I was shot in the head. I could tell something was off in his voice and I could feel his nervous energy." Ellie told her how sorry she was for what happened to her but also thought she should know that Robert also had another family back in London.

Kat said that didn't surprise her now, and she also told them she hadn't seen her children since. Ellie was pretty sure Thomas probably got rid of any loose ends, no matter their age. She said she was going to stay on the farm. Ellie ended the visit with her usual, "Thank you for coming forward and speaking with us."

The next visitor that came after Kat left was Thomas's daughter, Auriel Finch. She was just a couple days old when Thomas and Mary Ellen became a couple. Mary Ellen also had a son by the name of Hudson. Auriel's mother didn't allow her to see Thomas, as she had understood there was an evilness to him, but Thomas would catch sight of her and her mother in town and would make sure she had a new pair of leather shoes every year. Her mother, Maxine, was a seamstress in Stenton and was able to provide for them.

When Auriel turned ten, her mother became ill and passed away, so Thomas sent his men to pick her up, and she lived in a house a couple of miles from the farm in a house with Mary Ellen. She said she was evil.

When Auriel turned fourteen it was acceptable for girls to have suitors, so Thomas introduced her to his top runner, Joseph, age twenty. After a few months they were allowed to have private conversations, and Joseph confided in her that his duties there at the farm were to kidnap small girls but that he never touched them. Auriel was disgusted and saddened by it. Joseph had mentioned the conversation to Thomas, so Thomas told another runner to drug her so that she would pass out, and she vaguely remembers that he brutally raped her, hit her in the face and head, and killed her. Ellie was saddened to once again hear that one of his own children was dispensable.

Before Auriel left the visit, Ellie remembered she had some pictures and information she had found on the internet that might be linked to Thomas, so she held up a grouping of photos for her to view and asked her to tell her if it was indeed her father, but Auriel said she couldn't see that well, which Ellie believed was because of the injuries she sustained to her face when they killed her.

"Thank you for coming and sharing your story, Auriel." Ellie was saddened they had met another child of Thomas' that faced a tragic end at the hands of their own father. What a monster. "You are welcome back anytime."

Jack spoke up and said, "Do you mind if she hangs around a bit and watches the movie that's on the TV right now?"

"Of course. We don't mind." Everyone settled into the evening, Lauren with her girls, Auriel watching the movie, and Jack and Mathews hanging out like they usually did for a bit.

In fact it wasn't odd at all to Lauren to come home from the office and for there be a slumber party of spirit girls laying on her bed watching TV and enjoying each other's company like little girls should, or to catch sight of a face looking out a window at her as she got out of her vehicle, or someone checking out her vape device in the middle of the night and making it dispense the cherry-smelling smoke. It didn't start out so easy at first communicating with spirits on the other side. In fact, it was scary and unnerving to the Westons, but it was just as scary for those on the other side…They had all come so far.

Sometimes the house would be really noisy in the middle of the night. Ellie couldn't quite put her finger on it, but it would be spirits checking out the house and its occupants. Some were welcomed and some were uninvited. One night, Lauren was in bed on her laptop when she heard one of the twins making odd noises, and then it sounded like she was choking. The noise also brought Leo out of a light sleep, and they both ran in there to see Sophie starting to cry and gasping a little. They weren't sure what had happened until the next morning when Lauren and Ellie had their regular morning meeting with Jack and Mathews.

Jack was there early the next morning by six thirty. Lauren had shuffled into the family room with barely an eye open to say, "Dad is here, and he said there was a runner in the twins room last night, and he unzipped the crib canopy and was trying to choke Sophie, but a child spirit went flying in there when she heard the noise and chased him off. " Lauren was a little surprised and concerned that a spirit could put their hands on a baby and cause them harm, but she was thankful that the girls always had other little ones watching out for them, even if they were not in body.

Jack continued with his news. "There were several unwanted people in the house last night, so Mathews and I are trying to round up some help so they don't overpower us and push us to end of the dome, because then we would be pulled into heaven and not be able to stay here and communicate."

Ellie was frightened about losing contact with Jack. "Well please see if you can get help from others because it's important for you all and for us." Jack agreed and said he would be back in the evening when they arrived home and would give them an update.

Ellie nodded and tried giving a brave smile and told them that she loved them and would speak with them tonight. They were gone, and it was the start of a new day…

After a long day, Ellie rolled into the drive with some take-out dinner, and when she walked in, Lauren was standing in the bathroom straightening her hair. Lauren and Leo were running some errands with the girls when Leo arrived home. "Hey Dad, Mathews and Auriel are here. Dad says that they have rounded up some help and it's going to be busy tonight."

Ellie wasn't sure what that meant but was glad to hear they had reinforcements for whatever came her family's way. "How are you, Auriel?" She didn't want to ignore their sweet young guest.

Lauren translated. "She's fine. She has been talking with me asking me what things are like this straightener. . . ." Ellie smiled and told Auriel that she was going to start the movie she was watching the other night from the beginning since the TV would not be monopolized with cartoons all night.

The next morning when Jack came for a visit, he said he was worn out. They were busy all night long. There were so many orbs flying around the inside of the house keeping out all the bad orbs zipping around the exterior. He chuckled and said it was like a scene out of the movie and books series Lauren liked that had wizards and warlocks as main characters.

Ellie was clueless about all that had taken place the previous last night and kind of chuckled with Jack. He said he thought when you were dead you got to rest but he was working twice as hard now. Ellie didn't know if that was funny or sad but continued her chuckles, as that's really all they could do...Be kind and be happy.

Jack also mentioned that Miss Auriel was able to put up a forcefield around the house for protection that morning but that later on in the day they caught sight of a runner that made his way into the house before the perimeter field went up, and now, he was stuck. Jack told his family not to worry, that he wasn't sure when the protection would wear off but thought a day or two, and that they were keeping an eye on the unwanted guest, and the runner was certainly anxious to get out of there, so he didn't think he would make too much trouble, he was way outnumbered.

By the next morning the forcefield had dropped and Mathews was able to push the runner out of the house and to the end of the dome, where he was forced off the property and to where he should have been all along.

Ellie was still in awe over the spirit world and her daughter's growing ability to communicate with everyone on the other side. A couple of the spirits had said that Lauren was Sioux spiriting. She thought that the telepathy Lauren and Jack could do was amazing, but they actually tried something new during a morning visit. Jack had teleported him and Lauren to the local humane society to check on a dog they had dropped off that was wandering on their farm and picking fights with their dogs a few days prior. The dog started wagging her tail when she saw the Westons; that made Lauren happy because the dog had cried and whimpered when she had dropped her off at the shelter.

Ellie was sitting across from Lauren and didn't realize that her and Jack were on a field trip. When she tried speaking to Lauren during that visit, she told her mother to give her a few moments, and when Lauren returned, she told her mother what they had just done. Ellie thought that was so cool!

She then addressed Jack. "You know that there are probably a lot of spirits, good and bad, hiding out there on the property where Lauren's house is being built, that need to be approached. Jack agreed there might be others over there. He wasn't sure, but Ellie knew by bringing it up that Jack and Mathews would get to work on it.

She was right. Within a couple of days, when Jack and Mathews came for a visit, he said they were starting to meet some new spirits over there and would have some new visitors for them soon. Ellie couldn't wait to hear what all they had to say. That evening they had the first visit from a spirit from the adjoining property.

Lauren translated: "His name is Landes, age seventeen. He was Thomas's nephew. His mother, Gaylee, was Thomas's sister, and they lived ten miles south of the farm. Landes married his girlfriend because she was pregnant and they needed money, and the job was offered for him to work at the farm, so he agreed. He lasted seventeen days there until they wanted him to "break in" some little girls, and he refused, so they shot him.

Ellie was hoping he could give them more information about Thomas' past. "Where did Thomas and your mother grow up?"

Landes answered the question. "I am not sure. They didn't really like talking about growing up because it was a terribly abusive situation." Ellie nodded. It made sense that Thomas was brought up with evil. Landes wanted to hang out for a while and check out the house, TV, and anything else that caught his eye, and Ellie said that was completely fine. Jack said they would be back in an hour and a half or so with three young siblings. He warned his family. "They are still very traumatized about what happened to them." Ellie said she understood and that she loved them and would see them after bit.

Ellie got busy outside pulling weeds and mulching to get the yard in shape for their barn market sale coming up. Before she knew it, she had been out there for a couple of hours and thought she needed to check on the ETA of the next visitors. She did not want to miss them.

By the time she got into the house, the young visitors were there with Jack and Mathews, and Jack was narrating their tragic story to Lauren. She had just finished taking notes and handed her mother the notebook. Ellie thanked her. "Mom, they are still so traumatized by what happened to them, so Dad told me their story. They are very scared and tired, and Dad wants to take them upstairs and try and get them to sleep. Ellie told Jack that that was fine and that she wouldn't go back upstairs this evening so that they wouldn't be disturbed.

Jack said he loved them, wished them good night, and took the young guest up to the master bedroom to get them situated. Ellie began to read the saddest story yet:

- Manson, age twelve; Eli, age five; and Violet, age eight: Their parents were killed by the runners in front of them, and they were taken from their home about fifty miles west of the farm. When they arrived at the farm, the boys were forced to watch their sister get raped, which almost killed her, so they tried to run to her aid and were beat up by other runners. Then the runners stripped all three of them naked and threw stones at them until they were badly injured and then strung all three of them up and hanged them.

Ellie looked up at Lauren and said nothing and just let the tears roll down her face. Lauren didn't know what to say to her mother as she was also fighting back tears. They both were thinking the same thing; they didn't know how many more stories they could hear, but they knew it needed to be done. After all, God had chosen their family to help out the souls still roaming the properties in order to bring closure to all the bad that happened to them and to either help get them where they needed to go or the comfort to stay.

The next morning when Lauren came downstairs she looked rung out. "I felt so bad for that little girl; I could hear her crying all night."

It made Ellie so sad that they had been dead for almost two hundred years and they were still so scared. *What a terrible existence*, she thought. "Why do you think she was crying?"

Lauren shrugged "I don't know…Maybe because being in the house made her miss her parents more."

Those poor babies. Ellie was going to see what she could do to help them, "Do you think your dad will bring them back here tonight?"

Lauren nodded as she laid her head down on the opposite end of the couch from Alexa and dozed off for a few more minutes. The nights were too short, with the interruptions of sleep from the twins, to others sometimes forgetting Lauren could hear them.

The evenings were warm now, so Ellie and her family were starting to sit out on the big covered front porch and enjoy the view while getting caught up on the day's events. Sometimes Jack joined them. Ellie grabbed her evening glass of wine and strolled out to join Lauren and Alexa, who were already perched in their spots to hear yet another fascinating facet of Lauren's experience with the other side. She was whipping out a cigarette while beginning her story of what took place down at the barn when she went to let her dog out for exercise. This surprised Ellie because she didn't know her daughter smoked an occasional cigarette.

"You now when I was down at the barn, I leaned against the big walnut tree beside it and lit a cigarette, and something caught the corner of my eye, so I glanced over and someone was there smoking a cigarette with me. The cigarette wasn't actually burning, but smoke was rolling out of the end of it, and they would draw it up to their face, but I couldn't see who it was because they stayed concealed from me. Ellie was once again amazed by things that happened on the other side. "Did that scare you?"

"Well yes, I was paralyzed for a couple of minutes because they hid themselves from me, and sometimes that means they are up to no good, but also they could have been checking things out before they exposed themselves."

Ellie just nodded as she sipped her wine and figured that if they were up to no good, they would start doing creepy things around the house. It only took a couple more days before they started making their presence known but not seen. When Ellie got in from work that evening, Lauren explained what she had witnessed when she arrived home. First, "Mom, there were pots and pans strewn out all over the downstairs and shoes were thrown everywhere. Dad also told me he shut off the water spicket outside and said it looked like it had been running for three to four hours."

Ellie just shook her head. "Good thing your dad caught the water spicket on and turned it off for us." The Westons had a well with plenty of water, but it wasn't a deep well, so after several hours of running it would have started pulling up silt, making the water murky for a couple of days. Lauren told her mother she picked everything else up. They both were silently wondering what all would happen in the next few days, as well as who all they would meet.

In time, most things tend to present themselves. More new spirits were found next door and wanted to come forward.

- Pippa, age nine: It was 1841 when she arrived from Arkansas with a bunch of other girls. When she arrived at the farm, they were immediately put to work. Her job was to remove the clothes from the dead children that were killed. It was day two, and she cut her foot on a rock and developed an infection that killed her within the week.

- Azeta, age fourteen: She was shipped from Africa on a slave ship with people of all ages. Once they reached the US, they were divided up and sold. She was brought to the farm and lasted eighteen months. She was used for labor and as a sex slave, and she developed a uterine infection and died from it.

- Cynthia McCullough, age sixteen: Her parents dropped her and her seven-year-old brother off because they thought it was an orphanage and they wanted to give up their parental rights. She didn't know why. As soon as her parents left the farm, they killed her brother, and she was forced to dig a hole and bury him. She was used as a sex slave and she became pregnant and died during childbirth.

- Dancy, age thirteen: In 1837 she was kidnapped two states over. She was a lesbian and was there on the farm for a week and a half when she met a friend, Suzie. They were caught kissing and both were killed.

- Kim Li, age eighteen, from Singapore, China: She was sixteen and a half when she was lured to the docks by one of her own countrymen that said her father needed her (he worked in the trade and shipping business). But when she arrived, she was met by a black-coated gentleman who spoke English, and she was stuffed in a crate and eventually sold to the organization and wound up at the farm. She was sold to a family, and once she was purchased, they traveled up the road, stripped her down, and realized she was more mature than they thought and took her back. They killed her that night, as she was of no more use to them.

- Margie, age eight, from Singapore, China: She was stuffed into a crate and put onto a ship that was loaded with crates of children. They were considered exotic and worth more money. She didn't last long on the farm; she died from malnutrition. (She was speaking Chinese, but Jack could understand her and translate for her.)

- Etta, age thirteen: Her parents dropped her off at the "orphanage" and left her. They lived in the next county south. She made it two months on the farm until she couldn't take it anymore. She had heard a rumor that if you cut yourself on a particular rock you would die from it, so she ran her foot across it. She died walking up on stage to be sold.

- Chester, age thirty-four: He was an informant for Thomas, and if he heard anyone in the community talking about Thomas and his ills, they would be lured to the farm and killed. Thomas eventually killed him when he wouldn't rape a young girl. He mentioned that Thomas knew the judge in the county and had some dirt on him, so the authorities looked the other way and never came out to the farm, even when they received reports about horrible wrongs.

- Emmeline, age twenty-four: She was kidnapped walking along a path in the county. She lasted two days; she was raped to death.

- Dexter, age twelve: His parents dropped him off at the farm. He lasted three months; he starved to death

- Garnet June, age nine: She lived two county roads north of the farm. She was out picking wild flowers for her mother along the horse path when she was kidnapped. She was there for a couple of months and sold at auction. When the people took her home, she kept asking when she could go home to her parents, so the people realized she wasn't orphaned, so they took her back to the farm. The runners killed her that night. They took a large marble and crammed it in her mouth, breaking teeth, and she choked and died.

- Garrison, age twenty: His parents dropped him off at the orphanage at age nine in 1831 because he was below average height. He was used for labor for the first nine years in the front and then moved to the back for experiments. They took chain links and put them around his ankles and used a crank to stretch his legs. They ignored his screams, and a bone in his leg snapped and severed an artery, and he bled to death.

- Abraham, age twelve: The year was 1842. His parents sent him there to work, as they were told it was a work camp for kids, and they were starving and needed the money. He lasted a week. They wanted him to lure little girls to kidnap and he refused, so they shot him.

- James, age eight: Dropped off because his parents saw an "orphanage" sign hanging up in the county they lived in, two counties south of the farm. He was thrown into a shack with seven to eight other boys. They were separated and stripped down. Blond-haired, blue-eyed boys got put in a different group and auctioned off. He lasted eighteen months and died from malnourishment.

- Clark Tinsley, age thirty-seven: The year was 1838, and he lived two counties southeast of the farm. His fourteen-year-old daughter Clarinda went missing, and he heard about the "orphanage," so he came looking for her. He happened to wander onto the farm on sale day and saw his daughter standing up on stage scantily clad with her hands tied behind her back. He started yelling her name and running toward the stage when two men dragged him away and beat him to death. He didn't know what happened to his daughter...He was crying while telling his story.

- Eliza, age sixteen: She was from the county. Her mother's lover dropped her off, and she didn't know what happened to her father. She was there for about a year, and she didn't sell at auction so she was used for labor and rape. She thinks she was pregnant when she died from malnourishment.

- Lizzy, age nine; Reece, age seven; and Tuddy, their mother: In the year 1848 they were all dropped off at the farm by their father. There were men in black coats there that tied all three down and raped them all...They were screaming and crying. After the man was done raping Reece, he took a long metal bar and beat her in the head, killing her, and then next Tuddy was hit in the head. Lizzy stopped crying thinking that would save her, but after the man climbed off of her, she was not spared either. She had not seen her mother or sister since and thinks they went on to heaven together.

- Opal, age seventy-three: She was homeless and living in the woods for five years. She survived the cold by making a dwelling of sorts in the ground. She dug a hole about five feet wide and five feet deep and made a roof of twigs and vines that she wove together and made a thatched roof. She hunted and burned fire only when there was burning going on at the farm (which was often) to mask her smoke. They finally caught her and shot and killed her. She has been staying in the farmhouse for decades keeping herself veiled and hidden.

- Abrell, age twenty-nine: From the same county, just a few minutes south. It was the 1830s and he needed a job, so he went to the farm and asked for a job…He lasted two days. There was a little girl around six years old the runners had beaten and kicked, and he could see she was badly injured and probably had internal bleeding and was dying. They told him to rape her, and he refused, so they shot him.

- Julia, age seven: She was picked up in Stenson walking around town with her friends, Clarise and Etty. They were brought to the farm. She doesn't know what happened to her friends or her parents. She made it two months there. They took the clothes she was wearing from her and made her dress in something else, and they took her shoes. She cut her foot on something and wound up getting a bacterial infection in her foot and leg. It was very painful, and she died two weeks later.

Ellie could only imagine how many more sad stories from the other side there were that she would never hear because so many had left that horrible place for heaven long ago, but she was happy they were in a better place and safe.

Of course, with more information and more visits from victims brought more antics from the less desirable that wanted the Westons to know they were there to cause problems. Ellie was at work in front of her computer when Lauren called to check in, as she was home with three little ones with chicken pox. "Do you have a minute, Mom?"

Ellie always took time for her family. "Yes, what's going on?"

"Dad is here, and we were talking, and he said, 'Quick, grab a handful of paper towels,' so I ran and got some, and the next thing I see were giant cockroaches coming up out of the family room floor—about ten of them—and they were three to four inches long, so I was killing them as the popped up. It was something out of a horror movie."

At this point nothing surprised Ellie. "Were you able to get them all?" Lauren reassured her mother that she had. Obviously, there was someone unsavory they were going to have to deal with that had powers beyond most. They just weren't sure who they were dealing with yet, but Jack and Mathews were getting good at surveillance and finding the unwanted and apprehending them until they would agree to speak with the living. In the meantime, the family would remain watchful of everything going on around them.

For a few days, it was quiet, other than Jack and Mathews making their morning and evening visits and enjoying the pots of coffee Ellie would put on at those times. When the weekend rolled around, Leo had invited two other couples over for a birthday celebration for Lauren, with the thought of watching an outdoor movie, but the rain pushed them into the barn—which was just as cozy and inviting with the antique furniture already placed in there for their big sale.

Ellie had taken her usual sleeping spot on the couch with Alexa while the movie watching was going on, and all of the sudden Alexa said, "Mimi, look at that snake. Get it away from me," as she was pointing at it a couple of feet away. Then she made a gesture as if it were climbing up the side of the couch in her direction. Ellie quickly made a shooing motion with her hands toward the area on the couch Alexa was fixated on. Alexa seemed relieved that the scary snake meant only for her eyes had disappeared. Ellie had no doubt that she saw one.

By 2:00 A.M. one of the twins, Emily, was screaming her head off and burrowing her face into her mother's chest to get away from the awful frightening site that had her so upset. That was all the confirmation Ellie needed that there was an evil, unwanted guest in their house now. But who was it? No doubt one of Thomas's henchman that still felt loyal to his dead boss, sending out the message that the Westons needed to remain silent and forget. . . all that they knew.

The next morning while the coffee was percolating, Ellie discussed with Lauren and Jack that they needed to figure out who was behind the latest attack on their family and get rid of them, hopefully after they find out from them who they were and what they knew. But not all the evils were forthcoming with information. Some of them kept silent as they were being pushed to where they needed to go. After all, they still have to deal with Thomas in that dark, murky place.

Ellie's appointments and days were picking up, keeping her away from the farm until seven and eight o'clock on most nights, but that didn't stop her from walking in the door and jumping into her digging clothes to search for more clues and evidence from the horrible past, even if it was just for an hour. She was getting to the point that she needed to have a conversation with the sheriff, whom she had a good rapport with and had voted for twice, because she had enough proof of what took place almost two hundred years ago—from the bones to the medicine bottles and a box full of pieces of leather shoes of that time period.

The world needed to know what happened out there so long ago and the victims not forgotten. She felt it wasn't enough just for the Westons to know but also all who would carry the sorrow of all those terrible acts and continue to pray for all that were affected.

It had been several weeks since she had enlisted the help of her friends at the title company to research and help connect the dots with an abstract dating back to when the US government first sold the property in 1816. Mavis had phoned Ellie and told her that the search was completed and that when she had a moment, she would go over it with her. Ellie didn't hesitate and told her she would be right there, as their office was only two doors down from hers on the town square.

Before Mavis started to present her findings, she informed Ellie that she was glad that the job was completed because it creeped her out…Mavis had been plagued with terrible headaches, and when she was there alone at night working on it, her desk phone would ring and no one would be on the other end, and the buzzer would go off on their secured door and open and no one would walk through. Ellie was not surprised by what Mavis had experienced and was now confessing; she had mentioned to Lauren and Jack while at the farm that she was having the title company research records, and she was sure that someone overheard the conversation and repeated it to those that wanted the Westons and anyone else that was trying to expose the farm's past silenced.

She methodically went through all that presented itself in the records, which was what Ellie had already found through her own research. She was hoping the abstractor would be able to find something more that Ellie might have missed, but that was not the case. Ellie's "aha" moment would have to come from a different direction.

One evening Lauren and Ellie were speaking on the front porch with a couple that Jack and Mathews had brought through. They were there to tell all they knew about Thomas and the farm. Ella and Graham White had crossed paths with Thomas, and he had told them he was running an orphanage and needed money, so they generously gave him $250 and decided to visit the farm to see how things were going.

They rode an hour and a half to get there from their property in the county directly south of the farm, and when they dismounted their horses and walked around the large hill concealing the shacks and stage, they were horrified by what they saw. It was sale day, and all the girls were tied together and being marched up to the stage with not a lot of clothing on. They quickly understood the devious nature of the business. They briskly approached and voiced their objection, only to be shot. The year was 1847.

Ellie said her usual to the nice couple in their thirties: "Thank you for coming and telling us your story, and we are sorry for what happened to you." The Whites said they were ready to move on. Lauren said she was getting a sharp pain in her head and thought someone was trying to intervene. As soon as she mentioned it, Jack informed Ellie and Lauren that someone else was there and that they had to go.

Ellie wasn't sure who it was or how long they would be gone, so she decided to go ahead with dinner preparations until they returned that evening to finish speaking with them. Lauren stayed outside for a while longer, and when she entered the kitchen, she told her mother what was going on. "It's Thomas. Dad and Mathews captured him and are escorting him back to congress, and Dad will speak with us when they return."

Ellie just stood there with her head spinning. She knew all the latest antics had to be done by someone with power, but they had been told that Thomas was forever locked up in hell, so she didn't give him another thought…How silly. She should have known the spirit world was sometimes hard to pin down and understand.

After the fuss of dinner was over and babies were bathed and put down for the night, Jack was back, and he informed them of what had taken place. "Thomas found some sort of loophole and got out of hell. We escorted him back to congress and told them about all the terrible things he had done and the ills he continues to do, so one of the members put a hand on Thomas's chest and he dissipated."

It's as if his soul never existed, so he is now gone for good. That's what Ellie had thought the last time, but Jack assured them that was the case. Furthermore, why didn't the congress do that in the first place so no one else would have endured his evil? Even hell wasn't a good enough punishment.

They visited a little while longer before Ellie started the evening pot of coffee and laid out some crème puffs (Jack's favorite) for those to enjoy that came in and out of the house that evening. There were always new faces coming and going to check out the house and the living. Ellie understood they were always being observed, even though she couldn't see them. Lauren would let her know and so would Alexa. When Alexa would start doing normal three-year-old things to show off, like twirling and dancing or racing back and forth on the couch shrieking with delight, Ellie knew she was showing off for others—most likely other children that she herself couldn't see.

The next evening Leo was working late at a construction site, and Ellie and Lauren were watching the girls play on the floor in the family room when Jack appeared and said he had brought a special visitor…It was Grayson Mae. Lauren smiled. "I can't believe how big she is getting! She is as tall as Alexa but has long dark curly hair. Dad says that children grow faster in heaven. He is also telling me that she has decided to stay on the farm with all of us." Ellie thought that was the sweetest news and somewhat hard news because Lauren would also need to be attentive to both a child that is not living but there very much in spirit, with feelings and emotions, and to Grayson Mae, who was trying to figure out the whole spirit world herself.

Ellie knew that the girls could see her and were playing with their sister because of their smiles and laughter as they handed toys to the space in front of them. Lauren continued. "She is missing an arm and a leg, but when she was in heaven, they created a crutch-like apparatus for her leg so she can walk, but she crawls a lot."

Ellie wished she could see her granddaughter and hold her tight, but that would have to wait for now. Her mind also went back to the arrogant doctor that told Lauren that her child had no soul. In fact, it was the doctor that behaved as if he had no soul to gain but only wanted to help advance his medical career.

As the evening reached the magic hour of bedtime, Lauren prepared some sippy cups for the twins, and all three babes that shared the same space in their mother's belly all those months grabbed their blankets, and Ellie watched them head towards the stairs to make the climb to their bedroom that they were sharing now.

When Lauren came back downstairs, she said that they were all tucked in, and Grayson was curled up with her blanket on the super comfortable stuffed rocking chair watching an animated movie with her sisters. No way could Ellie, Lauren, or Jack, before Jack's passing, have imagined themselves living their lives today as such, but it was what they now had and what they were holding onto.

Ellie had another packed day and was on an appointment that morning when Lauren called her, so she stepped out onto the back deck of the property she was showing for a quick conversation with her daughter. "Mom, I smelled something that was burning and then all of the sudden the power went off, so I called the electric company, and they assured me the power was still on and had me check the electrical box. All breakers were in the on position. The woman on the other end said I had something strange going on. I also walked around the house to make sure nothing was on fire." Ellie knew who it was: Mary Ellen. After all, Thomas had found the loophole, and she was sure that evil woman was following his lead.

Ellie told Lauren to get ready and get the girls out of the house because she suspected they were going to have to deal with Thomas's other half now. When Ellie arrived home that evening no one was around, and as she carried in an armload of groceries and immediately felt like she was being watched and had a creepy feeling, but she wasn't frightened easily these days…She liked to hit things head on like a bull.

She called out her hellos to Jack and Mathews and then followed with, "I know you are here, Mary Ellen you evil bitch!" Even though she couldn't see her, she could feel her presence. It was just a matter of time before she would drop her veil and get caught by someone in the house that kept themselves hidden even better. Ellie and her family would just have to keep on their toes, and their adversaries on the other side would have to keep a diligent watch for Mary Ellen.

Lauren's seizures came out of nowhere again and for the next two to three weeks; keeping her upright was a challenge and safety concern for her. There were a couple of close calls, and Jack was there both times to spare his daughter from joining him on the other side too soon…After all, she had three young daughters who very much needed her, as well as her mother.

One of the seizures happened outside while Lauren was sitting on the porch swing while Alexa helped her grandmother pull weeds around the stone patio overlooking the pool area. Ellie didn't hear Lauren fall from the swing because Jack was around. When he saw his daughter going headfirst toward the deck, he was sure she would snap her neck, so he was able to catch her. That's why Ellie had no clue there was a problem as she squatted, pulling weeds and listening to Alexa chattering.

All of the sudden Ellie heard crying and glanced over to the swing where her daughter had been sitting, and Lauren was on the deck in full seizure mode. Ellie quickly jumped up and ran in her daughter's direction, yelling her name.

Ellie couldn't understand why she didn't hear her daughter fall or why she didn't hear her flailing about during the seizure. Furthermore, Lauren was completely unconscious. So who was that crying? Someone upset at what they were watching, but whoever's sobs Ellie heard, she was grateful for the sound to alert her to Lauren's needs. Poor Alexa stood there crying, watching Ellie tend to her daughter, so she escorted Alexa inside so cartoons would distract her, and she hollered for Leo to help , he was upstairs, tending to the twins.

It took Lauren twenty minutes to come to, and she seemed a little disoriented, saying she needed her dad and asking where Jack was. The last time Lauren had a memory loss, it took her two weeks to get back to them. It was a terrible time for everyone. Her parents weren't sure how long it would take for her to start remembering, and Lauren would look at her family everyday and cry, asking who they all were. Ellie wasn't sure if her heart could take another round of that, but whatever was thrown her way, she didn't have much choice but to accept it and deal with it.

The next round of seizures later on that day happened around 6:00 P.M. as their friends were leaving the pool deck because of a thunderstorm moving in. They were all standing on the back deck, and Lauren had been on the couch sleeping since the earlier round of seizures when all of a sudden they heard a banging on the glass patio door, and they could see a baby stroller moving back and forth, hitting the door. Ellie glanced down, and Lauren was on the floor. "Oh my God, she is having another seizure." Ellie raced inside to help her daughter. Lauren was already on her side, but her breathing was slight and rattling from the vomit that was still in her airway. Josh Taylor rushed in and lifted her up and turned her over so others could smack her back to help free her vomit that was in her mouth and upper throat area.

Chance and Mia had been poolside that afternoon as well, and when Chance came in and saw what was happening, he jumped in to help and told his mother to go ahead and call an ambulance. The EMTs were there in no time, and as they worked on Lauren, who was still unresponsive, they started in with their battery of questions as they loaded her on the gurney.

Leo had just pulled up with all the girls. They had been at his mother's house visiting. Ellie hadn't had the opportunity to phone him yet to inform him of what was taking place with his children's mother. He left the girls in the truck and came running inside to see what had happened. Once he saw that she seemed to be stable, he told Ellie he would meet them at the hospital after he dropped the girls back off with his mother.

As the ambulance was pulling out of the drive, Ellie remembered the last ambulance ride she had taken, and fought back tears at the thought of losing her daughter, but she had the feeling everything was going to be okay and that Lauren had dodged another bullet with her epilepsy.

The hospital trip turned out to be another typical run, and six hours later, Lauren, Leo, and Ellie were all walking out thankful that things had turned out in their favor. It was always a good sign when Lauren wanted to grab something to eat, even if it was after midnight and all were exhausted.

After they dropped Ellie off at the farm, they ran to pick up their babies to bring them home to their own surroundings. They all slept better when they were under the same roof. Ellie was already wondering how she was going to adjust when they moved out to their new home next door, but like everything else life had thrown at her in the last six months, she learned she had to adapt and accept what was in God's plan, no matter how hard it was to deal with.

The next week was pretty normal for the Westons—whatever that now meant— until Ellie's prediction of having to deal with Mary Ellen once she found the loophole out of hell like her husband came full circle.

It was mid-week, and Ellie had just came downstairs from taking her morning shower in preparation for her workday. When she rounded the corner to the kitchen, Lauren was sitting on the couch in the family room and said, "We have a visitor this morning." Ellie thought nothing of it since Lauren didn't seem too telling and assumed it was yet another victim of the horrible owners so long ago.

"Oh, sorry to keep anyone waiting." Ellie was always concerned about that, but Jack would have to remind her his side had nothing but time.

Lauren spoke up. "It's Mary Ellen." Ellie knew it was just a matter of time before they would be communicating with her again, but she was still a little taken back because Mary Ellen had been laying low for a few days, keeping her presence quiet.

Mary Ellen began to speak. "It wasn't me causing the seizures. Frankly, that takes too much energy, and I just don't care if you make public what Thomas did. He ruined my life." Ellie kept listening. "My parents didn't want me to marry him, and they were mysteriously killed in an accident." Ellie was so surprised Mary Ellen was telling a little bit about her life, she didn't ask her some key questions that might have helped with the puzzle of who they were. Where did they come from? What more could she tell them about the monster she was married to?

But the more Mary Ellen spoke and tried to deflect any wrongdoing on her part and blame it all on Thomas, Ellie started bringing up the horridness of her actions and firing off questions Mary Ellen didn't want to face. "Why didn't you kill Thomas and end the terrible things that happened out here and to all those children?"

Of course Mary Ellen picked up the victim role again. "I did try, and then he would beat me for it." Ellie wasn't buying her lies. They had spoken with enough of their victims to understand that she played a big part of all the evils, and she certainly had a drug problem and enjoyed the money and all the fancy clothes.

"There was a pretty twenty-seven-year-old. Her name was Deidre, and she was kidnapped by your organization and forced to be a "nurse," verifying if young girls still had their virginity intact and to help take care of the ill children. Your husband became infatuated with her and kept raping her, and she wound up pregnant with his child. You found out about it and stomped on her stomach, making her abort the baby, and then you proceeded to cut off her hair, cut off her breasts, and sew her vagina shut…She lasted two weeks before she died of an infection. Did you not do that to her?"

Ellie was surprised when Mary Ellen answered, "Yes, but there were women here wanting to sleep with Thomas."

Ellie started to lose her cool. "I assure you they did not want to sleep with him, but if they acted so inclined, it was because they were trying to save their lives, not because they were interested in that evil man." Of course, Mary Ellen was getting irritated herself because she understood Ellie still wasn't buying her shit.

Ellie continued. "And weren't you the one that murdered that woman that was staying in the cabin in the back with Thomas, and you took her child and named him Benton?"

"I didn't kill her."

"Then who did?"

Mary Ellen stated again. "It wasn't me."

Ellie became silent, pursing her lips and shaking her head. If it wasn't her, then she ordered someone else to do it, which made her just as guilty. "We know about a lot of terrible things you did, so you can deny whatever, but this is your last chance to be honest with yourself and honest with us."

Jack spoke up and told Ellie, "She isn't paying any attention to you at this point, and you are getting upset so the visit is over."

Ellie was disappointed she didn't get any more information from her. Why would it matter at this point for Mary Ellen to tell all she knew, all she did? But Ellie understood it was another attempt for her to deflect all the evils onto Thomas, but everyone understood she had a heavy hand in all of it.

A couple of minutes went by with silence, and Ellie asked, "Is she gone"?

Jack answered through Lauren, "Yes, I found her wandering in the back along the field and I asked her what she was doing, and she said nothing, so I told her she might as well come and talk. Now Mathews is taking her back to congress, where they will permanently dissipate her soul as if she never existed. "

Ellie threw out her opinion. "She was probably looking at the ravine and seeing how much unearthing has taken place." Jack agreed, but he really wasn't sure what she was up to. Mary Ellen acted as if she didn't care anymore, but they all knew better. She possessed enough power to move the moneybox around in the ground and maybe even victims' remains. Ellie was pretty sure it was her causing Lauren's seizures and cutting the power to the house, both of which she denied.

The calm had come back into their lives, and the Westons were appreciative of it, considering all the health issues Lauren had gone through recently. Ellie was pleasantly surprised when her mother phoned to say Ellie's brother Grant would be in town for two to three days and that he would swing in for a visit at the farm.

Ellie was looking forward to seeing her brother, but like Chance, Grant didn't believe—or maybe just didn't want to believe—there was life after death and that those willing could communicate with those that had left the shell of their earthly body. She wasn't sure if she would or could open up a discussion about family members that Jack had brought from heaven to speak with them, but after a couple of beers, she would see how his mood was and decide if she had enough nerve to try again to talk about what she had experienced and what she knew about the other side.It was Saturday evening, and it was rolling towards the seven o'clock hour when Chance pulled up in the drive, so when Red alerted Ellie with his barking, she knew her brother had arrived. Before she could finish tossing the pasta together, he was walking through her front door and met her with, "What's going on?" Ellie put down her large pasta platter and hugged her brother. He gave her a big hug with his bulging biceps. Like Ellie, Grant liked to go to the gym and keep in shape, even though he was also past the fifty-year mark.

"Want to go out on the back deck and throw back a couple of beers?"

"You know I'm always up for that." Ellie grabbed a couple of beers, the bucket of peanuts in their shells, and a cigar. She only smoked on occasion, when she would drink, and it was always a cigar.

As they sat out back enjoying the beautiful view and catching up with their lives and all that had happened in the last six months, the beers went down fast, and her hesitation toward feeling him out on his thoughts of loved ones passed and communicating with them lessened.

"So...remember when I told you we could communicate with Jack?"

"Yes, you mentioned it."

"We have also communicated with Dad, our half-brother William, and Grandma Ester."

Grant sat there and listened and Ellie continued. "Our brother said it was kind of weird because he hadn't been able to speak with a live person since he passed. He said that Dad was more of a parent than his mother, and he wished he would have listened to him and gotten away from the girl he was dating because she had a bad drug problem and it just encouraged him to keep using." William had passed from a drug overdose twelve years before.

Ellie had never met William but spoke to him on the phone after she wrote him a letter and sent it to the address their father had given her. It didn't take long for the private investigator to get back with their father with information on an address and college enrollment.

William's mother and their father had a nasty divorce, and she did not allow him to have contact with their son, and after she remarried, Lance lost complete contact with his son. Ever since William could remember, his mother had told him that his father was dead. It was a shock for him to learn that his father was very much alive and had tracked him down. His mother had passed away two years prior, and it seemed timing was everything.

Ellie continued. "Jack has communicated with Grandma, and she is alone in heaven. Turns out Grandpa chose to spend eternity with someone else, but I haven't spoken to her yet." That really didn't seem to surprise Ellie because she felt her grandmother wasn't overly kind to her husband. "Do me a favor, Grant. Write down some questions that only you and Dad would know the answers to, and I will have Jack bring him down from heaven for a visit and ask him those questions and then get back with you."

"Okay." Grant didn't hesitate with his answer. Ellie wasn't sure if it was because of all the alcohol they had drank or if he was actually starting to believe in all that he was told. Before he left that evening, he asked Ellie for a piece of paper and wrote down three questions only his father could answer, and when he handed her back the paper, he said, "We will see."

After they said their goodbyes, Ellie went back into the kitchen and read the questions Grant had written for their father: 1) Name the two musicals you used to joke about. 2) What does your most favorite postcard I've ever sent you say? 3) What movie did we see at the same time you (within a day) hit your largest jackpot ever on a slot machine?

Ellie thought to herself, *only Lance could answer those questions! Hopefully that would solidify belief for Grant and evoke curiosity about other intel Ellie could give him from the other side.*

A few more days had passed and things were quiet with Jack. Other than a quick "good morning," there wasn't much interaction, and Ellie was starting to feel a little isolated, as if she was on her own island in the middle of the sea of life and finding it hard to navigate through unknown waters. But if she was feeling that way, she could only imagine how Jack felt on the other side.

Ellie was thankful Jack showed up one evening and said that they would have a new visitor with a lot of information at around eleven that night. That seemed to help snap her out of thinking about her own feelings and bring her back to what was important: speaking to those that lost so much there and asking what they could tell the Westons to help complete the puzzle of what happened there with the jagged edges of truth.

The hour quickly came, and Lauren announced to her mother that they were there as she took a seat at the kitchen island, where her mother was finishing up the last of her evening chores. "Dad has brought Julius, Mary Ellen's brother. He was thirty-seven when he was killed in the first planned raid, which only six to seven men participated in. He was the first one that was killed at the hands of Thomas and the rest followed his fate. When he found out what they were doing there on the farm, he went to the sheriff and the judge in Stenson, but no one would help, so they attempted to stop it but didn't have enough men."

"We are sorry that happened to you, Julius." Ellie started her questions. "So the sheriff ignored your pleas for help?"

"Yes. It turned out he knew Thomas very well and came out to the farm often to rape whatever girl he wanted and to get his opium supply."

"Where were you and Mary Ellen from?"

"We came from the Maryland area. We were ages eleven and thirteen and were orphaned, and we traveled west to Indiana to escape being sent to an orphanage." Ellie remembered what Mary Ellen had said when she came through the last time: "Your sister said her parents didn't want her to marry Thomas."

Julius began his response, "She lied, we had different fathers my last name was Loom and hers was St Claire and we were on our own at a very young age."

Ellie really wasn't surprised by what she was being told. After all, when Mary Ellen made appearances, she tried hard to pretend she was a victim and not the monster she truly was.

"I will try and get as much information for you as I possibly can before I move on," Julius said.

"Thank you, Julius. We appreciate you coming, and stay safe out there. The property has been ridden of most evil, but there are still some that are still lying low that haven't been dealt with."

"I will. I will be back when I have more." He was gone.

Jack spoke up. "Julius has been hiding from Thomas and his sister, but when he heard their souls were no longer existing, he felt he could come forward, but there are still others out there that don't want him to tell what he knows."

Before Jack left the visit, Ellie wanted to ask him before she forgot, "Can you bring my father down from heaven? Grant wrote down some questions for him, and when he answers them, I think Grant will be a believer."

Lauren cracked a smile and nodded. "Dad says he will as soon as he earns more points because he did something he wasn't supposed to."

Ellie was shocked. "What happened, Jack?"

"When I approached Mary Ellen the last time, I wasn't supposed to be speaking with her. She was on her way to be dissipated by congress, but I didn't know that." Ellie found some of the rules in spirit world downright absurd. Why should Mary Ellen have any privileges, period? Her and Thomas's souls should have been disintegrated immediately and not allowed to come and go from hell and have the ability to intimidate those that they had already taken everything from. Where were their victims' rights?

Ellie understood that God had his master plan, and some of it made sense but she felt some of it needed revamping, and she voiced her opinion often to Jack. She figured she would be penalized down the road when her time came for questioning the higher power, but there were many things to the spirit world that didn't make sense—especially the fact that there were rules and you didn't have a handbook so you didn't know when you were breaking them until you had some of your privileges taken away.

It was pretty quiet for the next twenty-four hours, and while Jack made a couple of appearances, they were short, and Ellie sensed there was more going on than Jack was telling them. Her gut was usually right. It was almost time for Ellie and Lauren to leave the office for the evening when Lauren walked upstairs to her mother's office and said, "Dad is here and he has a lot to tell us, and it will take about twenty minutes. Do you have the time?"

"Of course. What is going on Jack?"

"I found out that I had a great-great aunt that died at the farm and a great-great-great uncle that had been involved in the operation."

"Oh my gosh." Ellie could not believe how full circle everything was becoming, and knowing how devastated Jack must have been to find out that he had a family member that was part of the horrible things that took place at their farm.

"I am still trying to find my aunt. Her name was Allison Weston. I will have a new visitor for you tonight, so I will let you finish up and see you later." He was gone

No wonder Jack was reserved for the previous few days and Ellie was feeling the way she was. Jack didn't disappoint. He was there that evening after dinner, Lauren started with her translations. "Molly is with us. She was Allison's shack-mate, and they became best friends during the nine months she was there. She was kidnapped, and it took two hours by horse to get to the farm. She and Allison were put on laundry duty and they were able to talk and bond while tending to their task. They had a blanket they put on the floor of the shack at night and laid next to each other...They didn't know when would be their last night. Molly died of malnourishment from intestinal parasites, and two months later, Allison took a dull vegetable cutting knife and cut a large cross in each wrist and bled to death. She had lasted eleven months. The year was 1843."

"We are sorry that happened to you, Molly. Please make yourself at home here, and if there is anything we can do for you we will certainly try."

"Thank you." She was gone.

"Jack, try and get some rest, and I am going to lay down on the couch here with Alexa. I am exhausted."

Jack wished her a good night, and he was gone. As Ellie laid on the couch trying to drift off, she started to wonder just how many more spirits were out there still hiding in fear. She knew the answer would come as time went on and as others were found or as they chose to come forward. Ellie thought back to some of the first spirits they had met and spoke with and their horrific stories and how they were now trying to help make their existences better. They did so by allowing them to come and go in the house as they pleased, taking dinner requests and discussing Lauren and Leos wedding plans aloud at the house. They were all invited and excited to attend a wedding.

The next day came, and that morning Jack was there with his great-great Aunt Allison. Lauren said she looked a lot like Jack. Allison went on to explain that her uncle Joseph had kidnapped her and brought her to the farm. He would go from town to town and steal people's money, kidnap young girls, and kill for the organization until one day he was chased down by a deputy in town that was not on the take, and he raced out to the farm to get away, only to be shot by Thomas for blowing his cover.

Julius was proving to be one of the Weston's biggest allies by tracking down other spirits and collecting new information for them, and they were grateful to learn all they could from their newest friends:

- Roger Walton, age thirties: He was in the first raid and perished with the other six raiders. After his life was taken, he remained on the farm and witnessed many atrocities: many auctions where the girls were begging not to be sold, people dying from starvation, the dead being taken to the river with large stones tethered to them to weight them down, the burning of dead bodies…

- Tudy, age four: Jack found her crying in the creek bed, where she had been hiding under a rock ledge for the past 187 years. She was raped, and when they brought in some new girls later that day, she ran as fast as she could to the creek, where she was chased down and bludgeoned with a stone.

- Drake Patrick, age twelve: His brother was a runner and was killed on the farm. Drake was recruited to work there; he built fences, worked on shacks…They wanted him to have sex with Sandra, age twenty-five, that they kept heavily drugged and used as sex slave. He was forced to climb on top of her, and when he looked into her desperate eyes, he climbed back off and refused, so they hanged him.

- Tex, age thirty-seven: Lived north of Stenson and helped with the second raid. A lot of people died that night, as it was chaotic and it was hard to tell who was good and who wasn't, so many innocent lives were taken unfortunately. When it was over, they gathered the bodies and cleaned the property so it could be sold. He came back a few years later, and when he stepped onto the property, the stress from remembering all that took place that night caused him to suffer a heart attack. He chose to stay there on the farm.

- Adelaide, age eighteen: Her father had a bad drinking problem and sold her to the organization; her mother had passed away when she was young. It took two hours by horse to get there. She lasted only two days. She was hit in the head and weighed down with stones and came to when she was thrown in the river.

- Joyce, age fourteen: Took five hours by horse to arrive at the farm; she lasted a year. Her job was to deliver poppy scrapings and liquid poppy to the log cabin courthouse and the saloon in town. She was always escorted by a runner. One day she got the nerve to write a note that said "Help" and slipped it into a package she delivered, only to be outed by the person that found it. She was taken back to the farm and shot.

- Fern, age sixteen: Her parents were abusive, so she came for refuge since there was an orphanage sign out, only to quickly learn what a nightmare of a place it truly was. She sold at auction, and when the buyer came up to the stage to collect her, she spit in his face. Thomas took her to the back of the property and put an axe in her head. She only felt the pain for an instant.

- Darla, age fourteen: Kidnapped from her home, it took a night's travel to make it to the farm. She was raped a couple of times, and when she went to the spring to clean herself up, she decided to run, only to be ran over by three men on horses.

- Little girl, age five: Doesn't know her name. According to others, she was there for about twenty-three days and was raped to death.

- Mason Greene, age fifteen: He was looking for work and was recruited. Slept outside with a canopy (tent) over him. He did farm work, and after being there for four months, he inquired when could he go home and when they were going to pay him…He was shot.

- Carter Haynes, age fifteen: His parents were killed and he was brought to the farm, where he was forced to live and work for ten years until they starved him and beat him to death. It was 1835.

- Berta, age twenty-one: She was kidnapped from a field while she was working. It took a day and a half for her to reach the farm. She befriended a runner, and she let him touch her over her clothes, and one night she slipped his knife away from him and slit his throat. Then she stole his clothes and cut her hair off and hid among others working down the road on the organization's property. When the body started to stink, they found the dead runner and then found her and shot her. The year was 1832.

- Libby, age ten: She was brought to the farm by her parents; they didn't want her anymore. She was there for three to four months and became very weak, developed a fever, and died. She wished her parents would have taken her to her grandparents.

- Shelly, age thirteen: She was dropped off at the farm by her mother. They lived in the same county. She made it almost a year but grew tired of the raping and abuse and tried to walk away and was hit in the head by a stone shot from a young runner's slingshot. The year was 1839.

- George, age fifty: His two daughters, ages twelve and eight, were kidnapped, and he joined the second raid party to try and save them, but they had already been sold. He survived the raid but came back to the property a week later, and while walking through the back field near the wood line, he fell into a sinkhole of about fifteen to twenty feet deep and it was several days before anyone found him. He had already died, so they covered him up in the hole. He has yet to find his daughters.

Ellie was thankful to all that came forward, as they continually learned new things about what all took place, and they learned the fact that there were more hands in the operation besides Thomas and Mary Ellen. She was beginning to think they would be dealing with evil spirits for quite a while longer.

There was comfort to Ellie in those sweet souls that encouraged them to keep digging for the truth and new friendships forged by those terrible events on the farm, and for those that chose to stay and create happiness where they could find it, which fell mostly between them all.

Of course, when new spirits show up so doesn't more of the unexplainable and undesirables. Lauren was usually the one to bear witness to such events, and then Ellie would get a quick reporting of them as they occurred. The latest shenanigan was someone letting in Lauren and Leo's rottweiler, an outside dog. Lauren would be the first to arrive home, and there would be their dog, sprawled out on the couch and no doors standing open, suggesting a door was not latched all the way.

Lauren didn't mind so much those quirky little things as much as the creepy vibes she was recently getting that let her know an evil spirit was in the house and keeping themselves concealed, which would make her extremely nauseous. One afternoon Jack met up with her in town and road home in her vehicle so he could have a private conversation with her, so when they pulled up in the drive, the front door was wide open, and she immediately got that feeling of wanting to vomit, it made Lauren instantly annoyed.

Before Jack could say anything, Lauren bounded out of her vehicle, ran up the front-porch steps and walked into the formal dining room and said, "Get the fuck out of my house!" The dining chair at the end of the table flew backwards, and the curtains on one of the windows did a dramatic swoosh to one side.

Whoever it was, they understood that she had had enough and was pissed. Even though they kept themselves hidden from Lauren and Jack's view, they must have been rattled by her angered demeanor, for all they knew, maybe she could see them after all. Lauren's abilities just kept growing stronger and expanding, much to most of the sprits' wonderment; they had never witnessed a living person with those capabilities, and it was a blessing to them, but for the evil forces it was a nuisance that made her a target.

Jack commented on the dramatic exit by their unexpected visitor. "Well, I didn't see that coming. Don't worry, Lauren. Mathews and I will catch whoever is in the house and push them out and to the edge." Lauren had all the faith in them that they would eventually catch the Westons' newest problem.

The wedding was drawing nearer by every passing day, so Lauren and Ellie decided to drive a couple of hours south of the farm to a wedding consignment shop that sold already-worn wedding gowns at a fraction of the price. Alexa of course was on board for that, while Leo stayed back and took care of the twins.

They had a hard time locating the shop. It was tucked inside an almost abandoned shopping mall with very few shops left in it. Ellie was starting to feel they had traveled quite a distance for nothing. Once they passed by the flowing wish fountain, Lauren and her mother felt a little more hopeful.

As soon as they entered the shop, it was a sharp contrast to the rest of the dimly lit mall with hardly any signs of activity. It was brightly lit and excited, soon-to-be brides of all ages were chatting excitedly with the salespeople as they scurried behind them to the fitting rooms in hopes that the armful of dresses would hold the magic one that made them feel like princesses on their special day.

Lauren was no different than any other hopeful bride there as she was greeted by Kay, her assigned salesperson, who would help her locate the perfect dress. While Lauren and Kay got busy sorting through the racks of beautiful dresses, Ellie and Alexa went to look in the children's section for a couple of dresses for the twins. When Lauren and Ellie were shopping during their quick trip to Vegas, they found a beautiful dress for Alexa that was a little pricey but so magical they had to buy it for the big day, even though a date hadn't been set.

On the drive down to the consignment shop they were talking and laughing about the mistake they had made showing Alexa her new dress that she insisted on trying on that second, but didn't want to take off and then threw a horrible crying fit when she was forced to. It took several days for them to convince Alexa that her dress had to be taken to a seamstress to have some beading sewn back on, and it would be a while before they would have it back, all the while it hung in Lauren's closet in a concealed bag.

After browsing through the limited children's section, Ellie couldn't find anything in the twins' size that Lauren would have liked, but she found the sweetest dress made of hand-knotted tulle, and the front of the bodice was beautifully crafted with big flowers with rhinestone centers. As soon as Alexa's eyes became fixed on the dress, she chirped up and said she loved it.

Ellie helped escort her to her own fitting room, and once Alexa put the dress on there was no turning back. Alexa had a second dress for the big day, but Ellie thought she could wear one for the ceremony and one for the reception. They both went to check on Lauren to see her progress, she was opening the current and shaking her head because she was beginning to think she wouldn't find one that day, but when she saw her daughter, that didn't matter so much because she thought her child look like an angel. "Oh my gosh. I love that on her! She could wear that during the reception."

"How's it going? Have you found anything that might work, Lauren?"

"No not yet. I am going to go back out and look at another rack." She finished throwing her top on, and they all went back out to the racks.

Lauren thumbed through the first dozen and then came across two she thought might work. Ellie thought one of them was "the dress" but didn't know how it would look on her. When Lauren exited the dressing room, Ellie was thinking the dress she had on might work. Lauren seemed pretty enthusiastic about it but wanted to try the other one on.

When Lauren came out with the last possibility, she was smiling and wanted to go stand on the pedestal in front of the three-way mirrors. Alexa was squealing in delight and immediately picked up the train of the dress to carry for her mother. Ellie was tickled that Alexa instinctively knew what to do, and she certainly got everyone else in the shop's attention wearing that huge smile and acting as if she was already there in the wedding procession.

The sales consultant placed Lauren in front of the mirrors and then grabbed a beautiful veil and place it on her head, Ellie thought her daughter looked like a beautiful bride, and she could tell Lauren felt that way as they both started to tear up.

Alexa was also beaming looking at her mother in that perfect dress she had picked out.

"Well, I think this is the dress," proclaimed Lauren, and Ellie couldn't agree more. The sales team went about packing up the dresses they found for the big day, and out the door they went. As they passed by the wish fountain, Ellie dug through her change purse and grabbed a coin for all of them to make a wish. Alexa tossed hers in immediately as Ellie and Lauren took a moment to make wishes they really wanted to come true, only to walk away in silence after tossing their coins in, both hoping their wishes would come to life.

The drive home was filled with wedding plans and details and all that came with it. When the girls arrived home, Jack was waiting for them and couldn't wait to see the dress Lauren had picked out. She unzipped the bag and carefully pulled out the dress that made her feel magical. Jack said, "That is beautiful, and I can't wait to see you in it." It was a stunning wedding dress. It was strapless, and the entire bodice was made up of tiny glass beads and the rest was flowing layers of sheer panels. Lauren couldn't have picked a better dress.

She gathered up the dress bags and ran them up to her father's closet, where all of his clothes still hung, and she slid some clothes over on a rod to make room for her future. The next day started a new week and another day of meeting new friends.

Thomas's Cabin Remnant

Doc's Cabin Remnant

Chapter Six
WAR

Ellie and Lauren arrived home at the same time that evening and Jack and Mathews were there on the porch anxiously waiting to tell them what had gone on in the last twenty-four hours. Lauren let her mother know that once she got the girls settled inside she would be right back out to the porch for a visit. Once Lauren walked back out and grabbed a seat, Jack began. "We found the runner that was hiding out in the house. He perished in the last raid. His name is Troy, and he had a bad drug problem; his teeth are all black, and he twitches. He was the one sitting in the chair the other day that flew backwards when we walked in the door, but he is gone now. We pushed him to the edge.

Mathews spoke up and said, "We have more interesting news. We met the man that owned the property across the road, and he will come forward and speak with us later this evening." Ellie couldn't wait to speak with him because she knew he might have useful information that could help complete the nightmare story of the past.

As the evening wound down with the Lauren's girls drifting off to sleep and dinner dishes being finished up, Jack and Mathews appeared and said their visitor would be there in five minutes. Ellie acknowledged the announcement and got busy putting away the leftovers of dinner and starting the next load of laundry, and then it was time.

Lauren said, "They are here…Dad, Mathews, and Andy Hale. Andy owned the property across the road and dealt with Jefferson, an employee of Thomas's who helped secure their covered wagons with dead bodies and ensure their safe passage to the river.

Andy then spoke of what he knew. "I didn't know at first what they were doing, but they paid me a lot of money to allow them to take wagons to the river, past the Indians that were camped on my property. They told me to tell them if they looked under the canvas that covered the wagons; they would have a problem."

Ellie was surprised by the spirit world again. In a book she found at the county library, she read that Indians in that area moved west around 1809. Of course there was no mention of the terrible crimes being committed or the so-called "orphanage" during that time.

Andy continued, "When I figured out what they were doing, I tried to put a stop to Jefferson, and he beheaded me. I was married to Bethaney Yates. Her family was from here, and we lived about a mile away with our three children. I haven't seen them since, but I think Thomas took my family after I was killed. After I finish this visit I am going to heaven to try and find them."

Ellie expressed her sorrow for what happened to him and his family, but she had already surmised that bad things had happened to Andy's family after his death. Lauren spoke up. "He is gone." Ellie asked if Jack and Mathews could find Indians across the way to speak with, and Jack said they would try, and the visit ended.

It wasn't ten minutes later when Lauren announced her father was back and said Mathews had found an Indian boy to speak with and that they would be coming through any minute. "They are here," was Lauren's cue to her mother.

"Hello, can you tell us your name?" Ellie inquired.

The Indian boy spoke up. "I am twelve years old and I didn't get a chance to go to the ceremony where I would be named…We were all murdered by the white men that came from across the horse path."

"Can you tell us anything else?" asked Ellie. "Yes, there was burning all the time, and the white men brought bodies in the wagons to dump into the river."

Ellie was heartbroken that an entire village was wiped out by that evil man and his organization. "We are sorry that happened to you and your family."

The Indian boy replied, "Thank you.

"Jack, can you see if there are any more Indians that will come speak with us?"

"Yes, we will see whom else we can find, and the Indian boy is going to hang out in the house and look around before he leaves." Ellie could only imagine how different homes now look to them and how fascinating the TV was to everybody.

By the next morning, Jack and Mathews had several Indians that wanted to come forward and tell about the evils of the white man that wiped out the last of their known tribe:

- Alo, "Guide," age thirty-eight: He said they considered themselves nomads and white people in town didn't know about them.

- Istas, "Winter," age nineteen: She was a teacher of the young.

- Keme, "The Secret Keeper," age twenty-one: His role was similar to a chief. He also lost his pregnant wife and three-year-old daughter in the raid. There were about twenty white men that came in at night with guns and swords, and they were all caught off guard.

- Mika, age twenty-three: He had just gone through his marriage ceremony the night the raid happened; the season was summer.

- Titus, "Medicine Man" age thirty: He said that the week the raid happened things seemed off with the white men. He also talked about hearing screams during the days and the nights. They suspected the people across the horse path were up to no good, so they kept to themselves close to the river.

- Chelley, age fourteen: She was a jewelry maker and also made headdresses. She slept in a hut all to herself because she sometimes worked on her craft after others were asleep so she wouldn't be interrupted. She was fast asleep when the men came, and they lit everyone's hut on fire to drive them out to shoot them, but by the time she realized what was going on it was too late and she died in her burning hut.

- The Chief, "White Elk," age forty-three: He and a few others were gone when the raid took place. They had gone looking for a new property to live on because of what the white men were up to, and also to hunt. When they came back the next morning, all the homes were burned, and their entire tribe slaughtered—men, women, children, and babies. So they crossed the horse path to confront the white men but were captured. Sacks were put over their heads and they were hanged. They were the last of the Raccona tribe.

The Indians went on and explained some of their tribal customs to the Westons:

- By age fourteen, boys would hunt and were considered warriors

- By age fourteen, girls prepared meals, skin hides, and they sometimes bred. Younger girls would help take of babies and small children

- When they reached age eighteen, they received another name Their tribal colors were golden yellow, deep red, and bronze brown

- They did not have a sacred burial site. When members of the tribe died, they would tether small trees together and make a raft, wrap them in cloth/hide, and have ceremony. The raft would be pushed from the shore, and as it started to travel downstream, someone would light an arrow and shoot it into the hide. Deceased children were handled a little differently.

- River, age twelve, Indian boy: He was stabbed to death trying to protect his mother and sister in the raid against their tribe.

- Ray, age twenty-five, Indian: His mother told him he was a ray of sunshine; that's how he got his name. He was a hunter for their tribe, but he did not go out on the last hunt because he was ill, and he perished in the raid.

Ellie was fascinated listening to all they had to say and heartbroken at the same time. It was mind blowing how many people perished at the hands of an organization that operated for forty years before it was taken down. After they finished with the conversation, Jack let his family know they were going to look around and check things out. Ellie assumed that also meant the Indians, which she didn't mind. After all, she was also on their side.

The chief expressed his gratitude to Jack for reaching out to them and to the Westons for their willingness to speak with them. "You are now family and one of us," proclaimed Chief White Elk, and Ellie couldn't hide the huge smile she was wearing hearing those words. Even though her family didn't die at the hands of the organization, they all felt raw and sorrow for all that had taken place, and they were all trying to deal with so many losses.

That week was full of visitors coming forward ever night to tell their stories as word spread among the Indian community as well as to the other victims:

- Ben Sayers, age eighteen: He lived about five miles away and was kidnapped and brought to the farm to work; he made it five years there. He did manual labor and didn't hurt any girls. When the organization was rounding workers up to prepare for the raid on the Indians, he caught word and knew that when he refused he would be murdered, so he killed himself.

- Lara, age twelve: She was kidnapped, and it took two hours by horse to arrive at the farm. After she arrived, a man took her to the back of property for "exams" (She did not elaborate; most likely it was gynecology in nature), and by day three she called the man a pig for doing that to her, and he said "I will show you what we do to pigs". He stripped her naked, beat her, then hog-tied her and put her over fire.

- Levinson, age fifteen: He was dropped off by authorities because his parents didn't want him anymore, and you weren't considered an adult back then until age sixteen. He was forced to work, and when he talked back to a supervisor, they withheld food for a day. The next day they put him in a shack with an older drunk man, who raped him badly. The next day they put a machete in his hands and told him to cut weeds and then they would come get him later and put him back in the shack with the man. He didn't want to be put through that again so he slit his own throat.

- Larissa Fenderson, age thirty: She was married to John Fenderson Jr. He was a part of the organization, and when she realized what was happening on the farm, she went to the authorities and brought them there. She quickly realized the sheriff was in on it when Thomas confronted her and then beheaded her. The year was 1837. They lived a mile north of the farm and she had a son and daughter. She didn't know what happened to them.

- Erin Wood, age thirty-two: Her husband Johnathan was a part of the organization, and when she kept pressing him about what took place on the farm, he brought her there and she witnessed horrible things being done. Then he shot her. They were originally from Wisconsin.

- Rena, age seventeen, Indian girl: The last thing she remembered was hearing screaming and guns shooting as men rode in on horses at night.

- Indian girl, age seven: No name. She said men road in on horses and they used a weapon that was rope with stones attached to the ends, and they would swing them around and hit people with them, killing them.

- Josiah, age fourteen: Brought to work on the farm with other young men and boys. They were loaded up in big black buggies and traveled four hundred miles from Kentucky. Half of the buggies were sent to the farm while the other half were sent to another location, and as soon as they arrived, they were put to work. It wasn't long before the organization told them they had to break in girls and rape and beat them as well as help kidnap them. They refused, so the first couple of days they withheld food. Then they withheld water and finally forced them to eat their own feces. They lined all of them up on a log and beheaded them.

- Indian girl, age nine: She hadn't been given a name yet. She died the night of the raid. One of the men captured her and held her until the entire cam was engulfed in flames, and then he threw her in.

- CeCe, age thirteen: She was a part of the tribe. The night of the raid she was taken captive and thrown in a cage. She was raped, and a few days later she developed chills and a fever, and when she couldn't stand up they stabbed her to death with a knife.

Ellie was horrified to learn that there was another location that most likely practiced the same kind of business and brutality, which meant the organization was much bigger. The Westons continued to listen to the stories and fulfill requests that were made by some of them. One of the Indians requested, through Jack, a corn-cob pipe and loose tobacco. Ellie was more than happy to oblige and was sure she would have to go to a bigger town to find the pipes, but she was ecstatic when she located some in their local smoke shop. The sad stories continued:

- Kyle McNatty, teenage cross dresser He was kidnapped off the streets of Stenson and brought to the farm. Once he arrived, someone was ordered to break him in, and once they realized he was a male in women's clothes, they went ahead and raped him and then killed him. Then they posted fliers around town saying if you have a missing son that was dressed like a girl…he's dead . . . just to taunt his parents. He preferred being called Katherine.

- Suzanne Walton age 42: Born and raised in the county. She lived two to three miles from the farm on a property she inherited from her parents. They were neighbors to Thomas and Mary Ellen. She stopped by the farm and witnessed girls screaming and being dragged to shacks. She was caught. They raped her and then shot her. The year was 1839.

- Caroline, age six: Witnessed her parents being killed on the farm and then they killed her.

- Janeece, age twelve: The year 1828. She spit in a guard's face because she was scared, and he strangled her. Once she was dead, he started to have sex with her but Thomas pulled him off of her. She lived in the same county, ten minutes from the farm by horse. She mentioned there were poppies everywhere.

- Christopher Jenson, age forty-seven: The year was 1839. He came from the southern part of the state after his wife passed away, looking for new start. He was in the area for three years when he got invited to a meeting in town. When he heard about all the terrible things they did, he alerted the sheriff, and when he came to the second meeting he realized they were about to kill him, and fear sent his body into shock and he died. They threw his body out back in the alley. The sheriff was involved.

- Nelson Samuels, age sixty-seven: A drifter, he had a wife and two children who had burned up in a house fire in Oklahoma years ago. He had come through Stenson looking for work. He stopped in a building in town and offered to clean it, and he was hired. He saw them bring young girls to town with their hands bound behind them and escorted into the building. The girls were brought in to show the men of the "secret society" what could be purchased out at the farm. He made it two months until he read through some of their documents and got caught. He saw ledgers listing girls that were sold and travel memos where some of the black coats traveled to Africa and China to kidnap girls. He was strangled and thrown in the back of building in the alley. The year was 1838.

- Tristan, age fourteen: She woke up on the farm and was not sure how she got there. She was there for two months and put up on the auction platform with her hands tied behind her back. At first she was defiant while climbing the stairs and then calm came over her when she decided her own fate. Once she was up on the flatform, she dove headfirst into the jagged rocks below, snapping her neck...She felt that was better than being brutally raped and killed.

- Indian boy, age fourteen: Men in black and blue coats rode in on horses twirling ropes with stones attached to the ends of them. He said it was terrifying to watch your family be killed in front of you knowing you were next. The raid lasted about an hour.

- MiMi, age thirty-one: After they killed everyone in her tribe and threw them in the river—even babies—they came back the next day and took their crops and animals they had raised. It was hard watching the white men take everything they had worked so hard for. She mentioned she loved to make jewelry and eat squirrel.

Ellie spoke up after Lauren had finished relaying MiMi's story and said that Jack's mother used to fix really good fried squirrel. "MiMi, what else can you tell us about the farm or what you witnessed?"

"There were a few men that ran the farm: Thomas, Franklin, Whitman and Lawrence."

Ellie knew who Thomas was but wasn't sure about the others. Were those last names? First names? MiMi wasn't sure...She asked if she could stay awhile in the house, and Ellie was always happy to get that question. It meant they were also curious to learn about the Westons and their story.

The week was flying by, and they had met so many new friends. Lauren was on her computer at the kitchen island looking at an online boutique that sold boho-style clothing with an Indian vibe to it. She loved the fact that bell-bottom jeans were coming back in style.

Looking over her shoulder and commenting on what they liked were two Indian sisters that had come for a visit. They were instantly intrigued when they saw what Lauren was looking at. Winona, age seventeen, and Aylen, age twelve. They had both perished in the raid with their parents.

The girls spoke with the Westons as they gazed at some of the latest fashion trends with Lauren and spoke about how much they loved and respected their parents. They spoke well of their tribe members, saying that everyone was treated the same except the chief and his family. They were looked up to for guidance and direction.

The evening wrapped up and Lauren wished everyone goodnight and slipped upstairs, since Alexa was already asleep in her spot on the couch and Ellie was quickly following suit. When morning came, so did all the goings on of trying to get ready and out the door. Lauren had walked down to the barn to get the dog leash Leo had left behind the night before so she could help put Red up and let her dog out. While she still had Leo on her cell phone explaining where he had laid it down, she heard someone walking around in the barn, so when she glanced over to where the sound was coming from, she saw a man she didn't recognize in a long black coat that looked like leather walking toward her.

Lauren's mind started racing and she started to panic. She knew that whoever she was seeing was not of the living, but he looked different than any spirit; his form was solid. She tried to explain to Leo what was going on, and just as the man got within touching distance of her, Lauren did the only thing that made sense to her. She spun around so she couldn't see him and braced for whatever was going to happen.

As she stood frozen and Leo yelled into the phone telling her to get out of the barn, she gathered up enough nerve and quickly spun around, and the unknown spirit was gone. Lauren finally responded to Leo's voice and said she would call him back. What made that whole experience so terrifying was that the stranger looked like he was a living person, but she knew he was not.

Once Lauren hung up the phone, she slowly backed out of the barn, turned, and ran up the hill as fast as she could without the leash in her hand. The dogs were just going to have to cooperate and listen to her commands this morning.

When Ellie and Lauren arrived home that evening, Chance was there mowing the five acres that needed tended to every week. Ellie was thankful for this, considering her hectic schedule, and with his help came the opportunity to visit. Once Chance finished for the evening, he made his way up to the front porch and sat down with his mother, who was trying to unwind from the hurried day with a glass of wine in her hand. "Would you like a beer?" Chance thanked her for the offer but said Mia was home cooking dinner, and he would wait until then to unwind himself.

"Thank you for your help, Chance. I definitely appreciate it and need it." Chance just glanced at his mother with a pleasant smile and gave a gentle nod. It was times like this that Ellie wanted to pour out every little detail of the terribles that took place out there on the farm and explain what all they had been through, but she could tell Chance wasn't quite ready to hear and absorb everything that had transpired after Jack left them.

They lingered on the porch a little longer, talking about things and issues that weren't too deep, and then Chance told his mother he needed to get home and that he loved her. It was moments like this when she wanted to say, "Stop. . . come back" to him as she watched him walk down the hill towards his truck parked by the barn. Watching the distance between them grow bigger with every step he took made her sad, knowing he needed to know what all they had been through and about their new friends on the other side. She wanted him to believe every word said to him…But it would have to wait.

Ellie was left there with her thoughts as she saw him pull out of the drive but was interrupted when Lauren stepped out and informed her mother that they would have visitors soon. It was time to get a few things done and the girls bathed and put down so they could give their time and attention to others who needed them.

As usual, the evening's visitors did not disappoint with the information they had to share. Lauren was sitting on the couch as her mother sat across in the big over-stuffed chair reading the news on her cell phone. "Dad's here, and they found out who the man was in the barn."

Ellie turned her phone on silent and put it down so she could pick up the pad of paper and pen sitting beside her.

"Benjamin is with us and he is twenty-five. The guy I saw in the barn was his nineteen-year-old brother Rogers. They had come from another state looking for work and crossed the path of Thomas and he and his brother took a job out at the farm. When Benjamin found out what they were up to his brother lured him out here and shot him. He is not sure what happened to his brother, but Thomas must have tied up what he felt were loose ends."

"We are sorry that happened to you Benjamin." Ellie always felt the need to express that sentiment.

Lauren chimed in. "That's weird because not only did his brother look solid form, but they made him look older."

Benjamin spoke up and said, "Yes, the dark side can do that."

Ellie had questions of course. "Where have you been staying since you passed?"

"Up the road about a mile in the woods. Word is starting to get around about your daughter's ability, and that is a threat to the darker side." Ellie was right, they would be encountering new visitors as well as the unwelcomed for quite a while, until all had revealed themselves.

"Benjamin has left the visit but there is a set of twins coming through now. Their names are Elizah and Ezeekial. they are thirteen and they were kidnapped from Africa." Ellie knew from watching movies and reading history books that they faced so much peril and despair before reaching this continent.

"Hello, can you tell us what happened to you and what all you know about this farm?"

Lauren started the translation for them. "They were sold and brought here and put to work immediately. At first they were fed okay and work was light, but within a few days they were separated and forced to work extremely hard, and then Ezeekial started witnessing men coming out of his sisters tent and realized what they were doing to her. One day he saw a man walk out of her tent fastening his pants and he lost it and ran over and started hitting the man. When they pulled him away from the man, they shot him. Elizah was devastated and died shortly after."

"They have been hiding in the woods over a mile away from here." Ellie was heartbroken all over again and thanked them for coming. Lauren told her mother she needed to check on the girls. When she came back downstairs another visitor was there and needed their attention.

"We have Ahammack. He was twenty-three and a member of the tribe . He says his name means "beaver." Ellie smiled and nodded and asked him to tell all he knew. "My tribe, the Racoonas, were wiped out by Thomas's men. We actually owned the property we were living on until the government took it away and sold it. We were lucky the man that bought it let us stay. Thomas approached us for about eight years asking us to leave, and we refused, so he got rid of us. "

Ellie expressed their sorrow for what happened to their tribe and then the last visitor came for the night. Lauren started shaking her head back and forth with a sad look and said, "This is going to be a hard one, and when she is done telling us, she will not speak about it again." Ellie nodded, understanding what they were about to hear would be difficult, and she was ready.

"We have Nellie Grace. She is fourteen years old, and she was kidnapped and brought here to the farm. When she got here, she was defiant, so a group of men surrounded her, stripped her down, and said she was going to take a penis in her vagina, so when she told them no they held her down and ran a red hot fire poker up her vagina. Then they told her she was going to take a penis in her rectum, and she said no, so they ran a hot fire poker up her backside. Then she said no to them putting a penis in her mouth, and that was the last word she said. They ran a hot fire poker down her throat and it killed her.

"She said she wants to sleep downstairs with you and Alexa tonight."

Ellie said she was more than glad to have her and that if they could do anything for her they would try their best. The last story was more than any child should ever have to bear and more than anyone should hear. Lauren and her mother told everyone goodnight, and not another word was spoken.

The next day at the office as Ellie sat there at her desk trying to get the day going, she broke down and let the tears run down her face while remembering the last story that was told to them the night before. Then anger came over her, and she realized that soon she would have to meet with the sheriff and tell him all she knew, what all she found in the ravine, and that she wanted those recognized for all their evil deeds. Even though they were all dead now, she wanted the world to know what happened and who did it, but she also knew there would be danger and resentment because there were descendants of those monsters living in their community now that had nothing to do with it and would not condone those terrible actions.

The Westons themselves knew all too well the heartache of having a relative that did such horrible acts towards others but had nothing to do with them, other than the fact that a bloodline connected them.

When Lauren arrived at the office later that morning, she let her mother know they would have a visitor in the office in a little bit—a man that was killed there. Ellie knew their office had to be connected to the events at their farm because in the last few months odd things had taken place such as thermostats being reprogrammed, pictures flying off the wall, and so much noise. Little did shew know that the men that wore the black and blue coats conducted their meetings there.

Right after lunch, Ellie walked into Lauren's office to see if she knew when the visitor would arrive and Lauren spun around from her computer and smiled. "Your timing is spot on. Our guest will be here in about sixty seconds."

Ellie nodded and took a seat. "They are here: *Dad*, Mathews, and Peter Nickelson. He was thirty-seven years old when he was killed here. The year was 1842. Lauren kept relaying everything he said to her mother. "He moved his family here from another state, and he had come into town to check it out to see what all was here on the square when he came upon this building and walked in while a meeting was taking place with men in black and blue coats. They told him to take a seat, and they finished up their meeting. He was invited back to the next meeting scheduled a couple days later, and after they were all seated a young girl of about ten to eleven years old and scantily clad was beaten up and her hands were bound behind her back. They turned to the new guest and asked if he could handle what he was seeing. He replied no, so they escorted him out the back door to the alley and shot him. He had a wife and two kids, and he doesn't know what happened to them after he died."

Ellie had a pretty good idea of what happened to them and felt bad for the man that he had wandered into the evil realm of the organization, and it was becoming quite clear to her that many town authority figures and community men were a part of it. She was amazed by how much information they had gotten from all the victims with every week that passed and how she originally thought it was just Thomas and his wife when really there were many more involved.

"He says that he is not the one making all the noise in the office. He keeps himself hidden. " Ellie told him if they could do anything for him to let Jack know and thanked him for coming forward. "Jack, how did you find him?"

"I came to the office for a little bit since you worked all weekend, and he was here and I caught sight of him, so I introduced myself and asked him if he would speak with us."

Lauren said, "Dad says he has someone else that would like to speak." Ellie was curious about another visitor coming forward at the office and wanted to hear what they had to say, so she gave a quick text to her client letting them know she was running fifteen minutes behind. She then gave her attention back to the room.

Lauren began translating. "His name is William McBain, and he is forty-seven years old. He was first on the list to buy the farm from the government, but when he arrived at the courthouse in town, people were acting funny and told him he would need to come back, so he went out to the property to check on it, and Thomas, who was in his late twenties , was there, and William asked what he was doing there, and Thomas shot him and wound up with the property."

Ellie told him how sorry they were for what had happened to him, and he was gone. Unfortunately her day made her keep moving, so she told Lauren she would be home with dinner by 6:00 P.M., and she was out the door to her next appointment.

When Ellie arrived home with Lauren's favorite fare from the local Chinese restaurant, Lauren said they would have another tribe member shortly, so they got the girls in their high chairs and dinner in front of them so they could speak with the other side. "Okay, he is here. His name is Cheyenne, and he is a fifty-one-year-old Indian chief."

Ellie acknowledged his presence. "Hello." Lauren instructed her mother to hand her the pad of paper and pen, and she began writing everything he said.

Ellie wasn't sure why he didn't want Lauren to speak aloud for him but instead told her to write it down and let her mother read it after he was gone. Lauren's writing started to quickly fill the page, so Ellie just waited until the pen stopped its motion:

"When the white men arrived at night in the raid against us, I was not strong enough to fight and was attacked from behind. I was stabbed in the spine with a knife midway down my back. As I was dying, I chanted and cast a 'curse' on them leading them to eternal hell so they would spend the afterlife on Earth until they were pushed into Hell…I now regret that. I had to watch my family and people die, and I couldn't move because I was paralyzed. I fell against my burning hut and when body caught,on fire,I didn't feel the pain because I prayed."

Ellie glanced up at her daughter after reading his words and said, "It's not his fault these evil spirits are here, and there should be no guilt on his part." Lauren agreed and relayed that their latest visitor felt like, because of him their family was stuck dealing with the bad spirits of the white men, and Ellie assured everyone that they were dealing with the evil because that was their purpose and that with everyone's help on this side and the other, they would push all the evil to where they belonged…hell.

The next couple of weeks had turned quiet, like a sleeping bear, as the season was slipping into late summer. Since Leo was working that Saturday, Ellie and Lauren thought they would take advantage of the hot day and take the girls swimming in the pool. So as they got them into their little suits, with many squeals of excitement from all three, Lauren told her mother that Jack had three teenage spirits next door that wanted her to meet with them, so she asked her mother if she would mind getting the girls into their flotations and into the water and told her she would be right back. Of course Ellie didn't mind. She figured this was probably one of the last few days to use the pool before it became too cool for girls to swim. Even though there was a retractable cover, the nights were getting cool, and so was the water.

Ellie was already suited up herself, so she wrangled all three girls into the shallow end so they could play on the steps, and as they got busy splashing, she heard the ATV fire up and go next door. The girls had been playing for almost an hour and were keeping Ellie busy when she realized her daughter had been gone quite a while. She was starting to get concerned.

Then she heard the ATV coming down the road and knew everything was okay, and she looked forward to hearing what took place. Lauren came out the back patio door onto the side of the pool and laid in the grass while panting. Her face was red, and as she was catching her wind, she started to tell her mother what had taken place.

"I met the three teenagers and after we spoke a minute, they led me, Dad, and Mathews to a location where Mary Ellen had moved a wooden box and watched guard over it while the digging took place in the ravine with the excavator. Once she got pushed to the edge, they thought it was safe for us to try and dig it up, so we crossed the creek bed and walked a short distance to the spot, and they told me to start digging.

"Mom, it was only about twelve inches deep in the ground and I touched the box. It was wooden with three metal strips across the top, and it was about eighteen inches long and ten inches wide. When I put my hand on it, I could mentally see what was in the box. It had some silver coins, old deeds, a ledger of girls sold and who the buyers were,a ledger of the secret society, and photographs with a device that took pictures."

Ellie was shocked. What a find to have that kind of evidence, but then she started to wonder why she was not included in such an important dig and where the box was. "So where is the box, Lauren?"

Lauren sighed and told her what happened. "All of the sudden out of nowhere there were yellowjackets darting in and out, and Dad said to run, so I did until I reached the ATV and jumped on." Ellie told her daughter they would wait a couple of days and then go back for it, thinking it would still be there since the evil person that had moved it to the new location no longer existed . . . anywhere. But she wished Lauren would have kept digging because she hadn't gotten stung, which probably meant the yellow jackets were an illusion conjured up by someone who was secretly keeping watch over them. It would have been better not to have their guard down either and to put a barrier around the area before any digging took place to ensure there were no interruptions by Hell's tenants.

The girls were pretty waterlogged by the end of the conversation, so they got them out of the pool and finished out their day enjoying their time together. It was about a week later when they had someone to watch the girls and they had the time to go back to the location where Lauren partially unearthed the box.

"Let's take the ATV over, and we can walk the same path that you took. Jack and Mathews were with them and guiding them back to the location. Not much was said as they worked their way through the tall itch weed, then across the creek bed and onto the path that was barely noticeable. As they walked away from the creek, the weeds became few, and the paths were very worn by deer running them. Once they took close to three hundred steps, a path shot off to the right, and Lauren said, "Here it is." They walked about thirty more steps, and Ellie could see a spot where the dirt was disrupted. Lauren questioned aloud why the spot was covered back up. As soon as Lauren said those words Ellis knew in her heart that the box was most likely moved, but they started to dig, and a couple of minutes into it, Jack told them, "Quit digging. It's not there." He had just received a message from Auriel, Mathews half-sister, who was still on the farm. She directed them farther up the creek bed, and as they walked they conversed with each other and soaked in the pretty sunny afternoon.

Mathews talked about how things were when he was living. The children would use berries and pieces of coal to draw on rocks. They used mudstone from the creek and carved their last names in them and put them out in front of their homes so people knew who lived there. They all talked about their favorite meals and about buying some fancy but simple dresses for some of the female spirits for Lauren and Leo's upcoming wedding, and about some of their favorite herbs that grew wild.

The conversation trailed off, and they each got lost in their own thoughts. Then Mathews spoke up through Lauren and made the sweetest request of Ellie and Lauren. "Would you consider getting a tattoo that reads 'Because of you I am free?'" Lauren and Ellie looked at each other teary eyed and smiling, and Ellie piped up and said that was a beautiful thing to say and that they would love to. Lauren told her mother that Mathews also requested that Lauren help him write it out so that the tattoo would be in his handwriting.

Ellie was touched that he had made the request, and she was just as excited by the gesture as Lauren. There was so much going on in the next couple of months, with the wedding, the barn sale, and completing Lauren's house; the special tattoo would have to wait until after those events.

A half mile up the creek bed, Lauren told her mother to go left up an embankment to what looked like a very old roadbed from long ago. When they hiked two hundred more feet, they veered left a short distance and stopped. "Dad says to start digging, so Ellie picked up her digging tool that had a sharp end on it and looked more like a crude weapon than an earth moving tool, and she attacked the dirt.

Ellie had only gotten in a couple dozen digs in the spot and Lauren told her to stop. "Shhh. Stop digging. Dad says someone is coming." They all remained silent and still for a minute until Lauren announced that it was Auriel again. Auriel let them know that she and others had found the man that moved the box and they had him cornered and were questioning him before they pushed him to the edge. He was also one of the owners in the organization but wouldn't divulge his name.

Auriel continued with her helpful information. "You can stop digging here because when he heard you coming up the creek bed, he moved it again, so we are trying to get that location now."

"Thanks, Auriel, for your help." Ellie didn't show it, but she was frustrated. "Let's just walk back toward the roadway until we have the new location." They all agreed. Ellie was still very appreciative of the time they were all able to share walking and talking, like a family would do. She just couldn't see half of hers at the moment.

As they neared the county road, Auriel appeared again and said, "He says he moved the box under the bridge."

Ellie expressed her frustration at this point. "How can these evil people that should be forever locked in hell be roaming about free to physically move objects?" But she wasn't really addressing her question to anyone in particular and was disgusted about the fact that not only life wasn't fair sometimes, but apparently so wasn't the afterlife. Jack assured her they would keep working on it and get back with them. The box would have to remain buried for the time being.

Later on that night, Jack was visiting when all of the sudden he said he had to leave. There was an emergency, but he would be back. Those words always made Lauren and her mother nervous because there were still many unknowns about the spirit world for them and the ones existing in it. They wouldn't hear from Jack until the next morning, and he explained what happened. "The evil spirits tried to force Benton to the edge and beat him up, so he is upstairs resting right now, and he said when he was strong enough, he is moving on to heaven. " Ellie figured that was some upsetting news to Mathews and Auriel because he was their sibling and they all died at the hands of their parents. They were all the good that existed in that part of the family tree…at least all they knew about.

Ellie assured Jack she was done bustling in and out of the master bedroom for the morning so Benton could rest easily without being bothered. "Jack, let us know if we can do anything." She was off for another workday.

By that evening Benton was feeling better, so Mathews escorted him up to heaven, which they were sure he would call home. There was a little sadness in the air the the rest of the week when Jack and Mathews would come for a visit, but by the end of the week, Jack came to Lauren and told her to tell her mother he had great news that Benton was healed from his ordeal and had decided to come back to the farm permanently. They all thought it was a good way to end their sad week, and the appreciation they all had for each other just received more validation by their staying together.

Lauren wasn't tired when she slipped into bed after getting the girls to sleep, Leo was already in his spot researching light fixtures for their new house on his laptop, so she gently pulled out a small feather she had collected and tucked under the mattress. Lauren laid it on her lap, closed her eyes, and cleared her mind for a moment; when she opened her eyes, she focused them on the feather and concentrated on lifting it up.

It didn't take long before the feather climbed three feet in the air. It caught Leo's attention, and he glanced up from his laptop and asked, "Where did that feather come from?" Instantly Lauren's concentration was broken, and the feather gently glided back down on her lap on its own will. Leo looked over at his soon-to-be wife and said, "Okay, now you are starting to scare me."

They both chuckled and didn't say one more word about it as Leo shut his computer and reached up to turn the reading light off on his side of the bed. Lauren tucked the feather back in its hiding spot under the mattress.

Her daughter wasn't the only one taking instructions from the other side. In the evenings Alexa would sit up at the kitchen island to draw and scribble as she mumbled like she was speaking to someone. Ellie noticed her granddaughter's artwork had an interesting look to it. She was drawing faces that a three-year-old shouldn't be able to master, and below it she was writing what appeared to be letters, numbers, and symbols.

Ellie started saving Alexa's peculiar artwork in her notebook that she kept all the spirit stories in. She wasn't sure what the meaning was behind the drawings, but her instincts told her they would understand it down the road.

Things kept changing and evolving with everyone. Jack had been working on skills and was way ahead of the curve, given he hadn't been dead a full year. He announced at his last visit that he could now conceal himself from others, which was a huge help when trying to combat the evil. That would buy him a little more time before they could sense his presence during a raid to eradicate those that needed to be gone from Earth permanently. The spirits that had been there for two hundred years had many more powers than Jack, but he was a fast learner, and they needed his help to rid all the evil that came at them and the Westons.

The newest visitors were still streaming in at a fast pace from all directions to tell all they knew:

- Sue Ellen, age five: She was sent to the farm to help her mother cook. She walked into a shack and saw her mother being raped by two drunk men. One was strangling her to keep her quiet and the other went to spin Sue Ellen's head around and snapped her neck. She hasn't seen her mother since, and she hangs out by the trees in the corner of the backyard where Lauren and Leos dog pen is, she plays with the rott-weiler at night…That's why he barks most of the night.

- Anna Belle, age eleven: Her parents were killed, and she was brought to the farm. She was there a year and couldn't take it anymore, so she slit her own throat.

- Laurel, age six: Her uncle lost a gambling bet and she was brought to the farm. A nurse became friends with her and would give her some of her food since she was so thin. She had a seizure one night, vom-ited, and choked to death.

- Jermane, age eighteen: His father was an officer under the sheriff in Stenson and also worked for the organization. He went to a meeting with his father in town, and members of the secret society brought their daughters (girls of all ages) in to pleasure other members. He wanted no part of what was going on, but once you attend a meeting there was no way out if you didn't participate in such acts. So one day, he shot himself in the building.

- Glenda age thirteen: She lasted eight days. She hit a runner, and they beat her to death with their fists. Her family recently moved to the area and she didn't want to leave their last home so her parents thought she ran away ,they backtracked from where they came from to try to find her…

- Redmon, age twenty-two: He was part of the first failed raid against Thomas and the organization.

- Chelsea, age eight: She didn't last long. They raped her and then hanged her.

- Morgan, age ten: She was Thomas's daughter, and she was kidnapped from town at age five. Thomas recognized her because she looked just like her mother. A new runner didn't know she wasn't supposed to be touched, and he raped her and beat her to death. He paid dearly when Thomas found out…He was cut limb by limb.

- Colton, age twelve: He was dropped of by officers from town, and they tried to make him a runner, but he wouldn't do the terrible deeds, so they smashed his head into a large rock and killed him.

- Tyler Rockovitch, age thirty-two: He was just as evil as Thomas. He killed at least a thousand people himself, and it started in a country now known as Russia. He was kicked out of his country. He met Thomas in France, and he wound up in Stenson too. He said he made Thomas look weak because his brutality was far superior, and he was one of the partners of the green coats, which was somewhat of a rivaling secret society. Their building in town was right next to the black coats. He claimed to be a cannibal and enjoyed killing little girls, cooking them, and eating them.

- Evan, age twenty-eight: In the Green Coat secret society building, he was made to watch when a wife, husband, and daughter of approximately seven years old and a man of about his age were brought in and strapped down to individual boards. They were not screaming, crying, or begging for their lives, but he believed they knew they were about to die (he believes they were drugged). They slit all their throats, and when they were dead, they raped the wife and daughter. He was killed in the building later.

- Natalie, age sixteen: Her parents were killed in front of her in their home, and she was kidnapped and brought to the farm. It was a five to six hour horse ride. When they arrived, she was brutally raped and beaten and then raped often there after until she became pregnant and of no use, so they killed her. The year was 1838.

- Carrie, age twelve: Her birthday is November 27. She was kidnapped and brought to the farm; it took two hours by horse. Upon her arrival they raped and beat her and ripped off all her fingernails because there was dirt under them. They eventually hanged her.

- Claudine Gonzalez, age twenty: She was kidnapped from Spain and brought to the farm by blue coats. Her father was wealthy. He was a silver merchant. She was raped and beaten and lasted six years on the farm until she died from an illness. She said men used pig intestines to cover their penises to avoid impregnating the girls. The year was 1833 when she died.

Ellie was amazed how many spirits were still there on the farm. They each had their own stories of brutality afflicted on them. For the past three or so months, she felt as if Thomas might still be around. She couldn't put her finger on why she felt that way, and she asked Jack and Mathews a few times if they were sure his soul was disintegrated, only to have them reaffirm that he was no longer.

It wasn't long after the last time Ellie posed that question before they delivered the shocking news that no one wanted to hear. One morning, Lauren was getting ready to leave for the office. Her grandmother had already picked up the girls to watch them at her house a few miles up the road when she heard glass break in the bathroom.

Lauren immediately ran in to investigate the noise, only to hear someone scurrying around in the upstairs den just off the bathroom that was currently being used for storage for her young family. When she rounded the doorway and looked towards the mattress and box springs leaning against the wall, they were moving as if someone was crawling between them. She yelled out, "I know you are fucking here!"

As soon as those words left her mouth, the cabinets in the hallway just outside the den were opened and slammed shut so hard that Lauren was sure she would see them busted because they were shut so hard, but to her surprise they were still intact—unlike her nerves. She felt extremely uneasy at that point, so she gathered her makeup and a baseball cap and out the door she went because she did not feel safe. Her father and Mathews were not around when all that took place, and she wasn't sure who she was dealing with.

When Lauren got to the office, she ran upstairs to tell her mother what had happened, and when she went in and sat down, she announced that her father had also arrived at the office. She mentally sent him a message saying she needed his help while she was fleeing the house.

"Oh my God." Lauren started shaking her head back and forth in disbelief and then started telling her mother what she had just learned from her father.

"It's Thomas. Dad says he is still here on Earth. They caught him in the house. He was the one that broke the glass and was making all the noise."

Ellie was shocked. "How can that evil man still be walking the Earth, and how can that be when you witnessed his soul being dissipated right in front of you?" Lauren repeated her father's words. Dad says they don't know but are working on finding the answers and will hopefully have some information for us when we get home.

Ellis just nodded, and Lauren said she needed to get some things done before she left the office. There wasn't anything either of them could do at the moment, and it's not like they weren't used to the curveballs that were thrown their direction from the spirit world...They would have to wait for the answers.

It was another long day for Ellie. She picked up some pizzas on the way home so she could give her attention to those that hopefully held the answers and not be distracted by bubbling pots of dinner makings. When she walked in, of course the girls all ran to her yelling "MiMi! MiMi!" which made her heart full. She was going to miss that sweet greeting when they were moved in next door.

Once Lauren got the girls in their highchairs and dinner in front of them, she made her way back to the kitchen island, sat down, and said her usual, "Dad, Andrews and the chief are here, and they have information for us. Also, a barrier has been put up so we can speak without anyone else hearing. They are saying that Thomas cloned one of his men to look like him, so when he went before congress, it wasn't actually Thomas."

It was starting to make sense to Ellie. The last time Thomas popped in for a visit to dissuade her from unearthing the truth in the ravine and letting the story out to the public, his demeanor and tone wasn't so menacing and he seemed resolved to his fate. It wasn't Thomas at all but one of his henchmen that was being forced to take the punishment; that's why he seemed different to her when he was speaking with them that last time.

"Dad also says that Thomas has transformed himself to look like him, and when we were speaking to him and Matthew wasn't around, that most likely wasn't Dad but Thomas." Ellie's head was spinning. How could God allow his victims and the Westons to be victimized all over again by this man?

Lauren kept repeating the bad news. "Dad also says that Thomas pushed Auriel over the boundary, which instantly moved her to heaven because she had extra powers, and he didn't like her working against her father. They are going to see if they can get her back if this is where she wants to be. The chief wants me to tell you he has some of his tribe upstairs and they are cleansing the house for us."

Ellie was glad the chief was forming a bond with her husband and family. She felt safer knowing the tribe was behind them and their quest to destroy Thomas for good so that everyone else can have a peaceful eternity, especially those that had everything taken from them.

The next few days were made up of the same, with Thomas entering the house once Jack and Matthews would leave to take care of others under their care and make the house smell of a strong ammonia smell like animal urine, and then in the evening the Indians would come and cleanse the house while the Westons applied calming citrus oils to themselves and their room diffusers. It turns out that evil spirits don't like such smells, as it makes them nauseous, and it keeps them at bay for a while.

Ellie also kept up her vigilant prayers for Auriel's return to the farm. After all, she was wanted and needed there by many and was an asset to the cause of ridding the evil that still lurked in the woods on the farm.

The week found its way to Friday evening and Leo and the girls were out for the evening visiting family. Lauren stayed behind, telling Leo that she and her mother needed to work on wedding details, and he was more than happy to let them do that if he didn't have to help with every decision to be made for the event.

Ellie walked in, and the house was already quiet. Lauren was sitting on the couch waiting for her mother and had a sad look on her face. "Matthews says he hasn't seen Dad for several hours, and we are all concerned that Thomas might have something to do with it. He is going to check the property boundaries and will be back."

"Don't worry, Lauren. I'm sure your father is okay." But deep down she was nervous because no one was sure of what all Thomas was capable of. Obviously they had underestimated his abilities. It was just a few minutes later when Lauren spoke up and said, "Matthews found Dad. Thomas had kidnapped him and held him captive in the woods in the back corner where the old roadway is that we walked the other day. Dad says he is shaken up and it was terrifying. He wasn't sure what was going to happen to him, and Thomas just kept telling him all the awful things he was going to do to our family and make Dad watch."

"Dad said he doesn't want to talk about it tonight and he needs to go up-stairs and rest for a while."

"Okay Jack. We are so glad you are back home with us. We will be down here if you need anything." It was times like this that Ellie wished she could lay her own eyes on him again, but that hadn't happened since the night of the TV sighting she had of her husband. But like everything else in time, it would come to them.

Matthews, the chief, and some of the chief's family helped keep watch over the Westons inside and outside of the house that night so they could ensure everyone got some rest and finish formulating their plan to rid the Earth of Thomas forever.

Saturday was dictated by the usual demands of daily life and all that needed to be done around the farm, and at around 4:00 P.M. that day, Ellie was done with chores and popped open a cold beer, with another following as soon as she sipped the last drop of the first. An hour later Lauren found her mother on the front porch lost in thought. "Dad says they have formulated a plan if you will come inside to talk."

Ellie jumped up from her comfortable chair, and as soon as they walked in the house a barrier was thrown up to protect all they had to say and plan. "Dad is saying they want you to go back to where he was taken in the woods and bring the metal detector and digging tool and to call me on the phone and act like you were given bad intel and that you are irritated with the good spirits...."

"Okay, I can do that. Just let me know when." Lauren repeated Jack's answer. "After you drink your beer, then you should go because it is getting late in the day." Ellie nodded, chugged her beer for a quick buzz and to expedite their plan, and she was out the door.

Ellie threw on her rubber boots and jumped on the ATV. The metal detector and her digging tool already laid in the bed of the terrain vehicle. She zipped off to the back corner of the woods. Once she arrived at the back of the property, she placed a call to her mother. She jumped out of the vehicle and leaned against the front so Thomas and anyone else back there keeping him company could see her and listen to the conversation. Before Ellie hung up with her mother, she casually mentioned she was getting ready to enter the woods where some trusted spirits told her she needed to go to dig and said, " I am not sure I trust the information I was given." She said this so she could plant the seed that maybe she was double-crossed and not very trusting of the good side.

After Ellie hung up the phone, she walked to the back of the ATV and pulled out what she needed and headed for the woods. She really didn't feel any different than she did when she was working in the ravine. She knew she had eyes on her but felt somewhat safe because physical harm had not come her way and wasn't sure it would.

Ellie walked into the woods and stopped after a couple hundred steps and positioned the metal detector in one arm and leaned her weapon-looking digger against the tree. She then turned on the device to hear the squawking sound it made when you first fire it up. Then she put it towards the ground, swinging it slowly back and forth about two to three inches from the ground, and started walking.

She had covered quite a bit of ground, the radius half the size of a football field when she decided to turn it off and set it down so she could pull her cell phone out of her pants pocket to take some pictures. Even though she couldn't see anything or anyone, she felt like they were there, so she held her phone up in front of her and started snapping pictures. She made her way 360 degrees around and, once she was finished she picked up her device and walked towards the tree to collect her tool, and then back out to the open field where it felt a little less intimidating.

Ellie next fired up the ATV and headed toward the ravine. That wasn't part of the plan, but if anyone was watching, she always stopped there, even if just to look over it and not put her hands in motion. It gave her a chance to remind whoever was watching that she was still after the truth . . . good or bad. Then she headed back toward the house, put the vehicle in park down below the house, as Lauren was walking down toward the barns with a smile on her face.

Her mother wasn't sure what had just happened. As Ellie got out of the vehicle, Lauren quickly explained that the plan worked. Ellie had no idea what she was talking about because she thought her exercise was the precursor to their next plan of attack.

"Mom, they got Thomas. Dad and the chief veiled themselves and followed you back there, and they were able to throw up a special barrier, and once Thomas touched it he was pushed to the other side forever." Ellie then realized she had been sent in with no knowledge of what was about to take place so that Thomas wouldn't suspect anything or read her mind, and it worked.

"How did they know how to do that barrier?"

Lauren repeated what was said to her. "The chief saw it done once and thought it might work. Aren't you excited?"

"Absolutely!" Ellie answered. But she had a feeling in her gut that things weren't over…Her gut instinct was usually right. She didn't want to spoil everyone's proud moment, so she didn't mention the feeling she had. There was celebrating to do.

Lauren and her mother walked arm in arm back up towards the house, and they both grabbed a beer and sat in kitchen and reflected on what had just happened. "Dad also wants me to tell you Auriel's back from heaven. She has been stripped of her thoughts and is kind of like an infant learning to think, and survive here on Earth again." Yet one more crazy thing in the spirit world for Ellie to wrap her mind around, but once she thought about it, she kind of understood why it would be necessary to delete all thoughts in Auriel's mind of what happened to her on Earth so she felt nothing but happiness...After all, wasn't that what heaven was about?

Ellie wasn't sure if it was Jack's negotiating skills, her prayers, or the fact that Thomas was pushed off for good that brought Auriel back, but that question wasn't nearly as important as why Ellie felt the way she did with the nagging feeling of the other shoe dropping.

The next morning that feeling was still looming in the back of Ellie's mind, and it did not go unnoticed by Jack and Mathews. When Lauren came down stairs to fetch a cup of coffee before the twins woke, she asked her mother what was wrong. "What are you talking about?" Lauren let her mother know it wasn't her asking, so she let it out what was bothering her.

"Are you sure Thomas is gone for good?"

"Yes, Mom. Even the chief is telling us that."

Ellie was getting used to having a full house in the morning. Now the chief was often with Jack and Mathews for their morning family meetings. She continued with her thoughts. "I just have this overwhelming feeling that it's not over."

"Okay, I will tell her...Mom, don't freak out, but there is another partner to the organization that we are going to have to deal with, and he is as bad as Thomas."

Ellie now understood why she had those vibes, because there was more, and she realized there would always be more. She was just hoping for a brief reprieve, but she was in it for the haul like everyone else.

"Dad wanted me to tell you that we will have some girls come forward with some valuable information on who we are dealing with now. They were killed in our office building.

Ellie said thank you and everyone got on with their day until their next meeting was to take place, so Ellie decided to make the most of the good weather and work outside pulling weeds and throwing down mulch so that her landscaping would look good near summer's end and into the fall.

After three hours of work, Ellie took a break and pulled out her phone to check work emails. While she had it out, she thought she would flip back through the photos she had taken in the woods to see if she could see anything. At first glance, the photos looked like there was nothing out of the norm— trees, foliage, and undergrowth—but when she blew one of the photos up, she was surprised at how many spirit faces she saw, and as she scrolled up the tree lines she saw the scariest demon image staring back at her. It was then that she realized just how much help Thomas had and how dangerous her going into the woods might have been. Ellie stood there staring back at the picture, not believing she had snapped the image, when Lauren stepped out on the front porch and startled Ellie from her gaze.

"Dad is here with the girls. Can you come in and speak now?" Ellie replied that she would be right in and gave her phone one last glance before she tucked it back in her back pocket and headed for the house.

Lauren was seated on the couch, so Ellie quickly washed her hands at the kitchen sink, picked up her notebook and pen, and then took a seat across from her daughter. "Who is with us?"

Lauren started the introduction. "We have Samantha, age thirteen. She is the daughter of Eddie Larrell. He is the partner we are dealing with now.

He came from Ireland, and he was part of a gang. She says her father sold her, and she was bought by someone that raped and strangled her."

"We are sorry that happened to you, Samantha." Just like Thomas, her father had no problem murdering his own or handing his own child off to someone that would bring a tragic end to a young life. Lauren announced that the next girl coming forward had a lot of good information.

"Nathallia, age thirteen, is here. Her father was the one that built the buildings on the west side of the square *in* Stenson. It took him two years to complete them, and when he was finished, Thomas killed him and took ownership of them. Nathallia and two others were shot in our office building when they were found hiding there."

Lauren kept relaying all that she said. "Her spirit has been there since, and she watched every meeting, rape, and murder that took place behind the building's storefront. She said our building was a men's store and it sold things men needed: tools, clothing, tobacco . . . and the meetings took place in the back of the building. Meetings would take place on Tuesdays and Fridays and sometimes the last Sunday of the month. She heard the black coats talk about picking up girls from docks in Chicago and New York. When they brought new girls into the building, the men would all say *carpe diem*. Ellie thought the word was probably Latin but didn't know what it meant, so she quickly pulled out her phone and typed in the word and read it aloud. "It means to seize the day. The saying is used to urge someone to make the most of the present time and give little thought to the future."

Nathallia continued. "They would also say a phrase, 'Two eyes are better than one, but in our brotherhood, one eye is better than all.'" Ellie hadn't heard that phrase before but it was quite obvious it was used by the secret society of men. Their newest spirit friend had also bore witness to events on the farm, since the partners not only owned the buildings in town but also all the land they acquired, whether legitimately, stealing or murder. The spirits could move freely on all they owned . . . good and bad spirits.

She continued. "Some of the men had weird fetishes; some would wear makeup and others would slit the throats of dogs, drain and save the blood, and then throw the dead dogs in the river."

Lauren and Ellie were thinking the same thing. If she saw all the meetings, then she knew who all the players were, and before Ellie could inquire, Lauren asked, "How many partners were involved?"

"There were about a dozen, but most of them were killed by Thomas." Lauren told her mother that Nathallia would be back later when she had more information, and Ellie thanked their young guest and looked forward to all she had to reveal.

Lauren chimed in and said, "There is another girl here that wants to speak with us."

"What is her name?"

Lauren told her mother that the girls name was Rosalie, she is sixteen. "She says she was kidnapped from Ireland at age thirteen and brought over to America and wound up out at the farm. Her parents were wealthy, and she wore nice clothes, but once she arrived they stripped her of her clothes and dressed her in clothes made from feed sacks."

"The year was 1813, and she was forced to do garden work and was fed every other day. She was forced to live with one of the partners in town. His name was Peter, and he was in his late thirties. One day while she was working on the farm, she was raped and killed. She made it three long years out there."

"The men were part of an Irish gang and they would tell families in Ireland they needed to send their children to America so they would not fall victim to the potato famine and the plague…They played on their emotions about helping to save their children when really it was about them getting their hands on children for the sex trade they had going."

Just when Ellie thought she almost had all the pieces to the puzzle put together, another spirit showed up to tell their story and bring new information. There were several partners. The girls were not only kidnapped locally but abroad. How could so many give so little thought to life and God? Who were these people?

After speaking with the latest spirits, it appeared the organization had been operating since 1813 and that Thomas had infiltrated the group in the mid-1820s and was not the founding father.

Over the next few days, Jack, Mathews, and the chief were around and would have brief conversations with Lauren and Ellie, but they kept their plans secret. There was always the unseen hanging around to pick up any information they heard and pass along to the evils. Ellie had jumped in her vehicle to head to work one morning, and her cell phone rang as she pulled out of the drive. It was Lauren.

"I wanted to let you know that a spirit is in the truck with you. Dad and Mathews are also with you. They are going to talk to him and find out what is going on, and I will call you back in a minute. Ellie wasn't sure what to think, but she had to assume this wasn't the first time an unknown spirit had hitched a ride, unbeknownst to her.

Her cell phone rang a couple minutes later, and Lauren told her mother what all they had found out from the stranger. "His name is Callahan and he worked in the organization. He dealt with ransoms for wealthy girls. He is saying sometimes parents paid, and sometimes they didn't care and told them to keep the girls. He claims he never raped or killed anybody, but he wanted to warn us about Eddie and that he was trying to round up help to attack us and that Eddie can take on solid form and pass us on the street and we would never know. He says that Eddie killed him and to remember the numbers 3862149."

Ellie was unnerved by hearing he could take solid form, and in fact that made sense. Just the day before Lauren was home alone with the girls for several hours and someone kept knocking loudly on the door, but when she would open it no one was there. Some of the spirits that were around at the time said there was a man at the door, but now Ellie understood that it was probably Eddie.

Later that evening when Ellie arrived home, Lauren stepped outside to announce they had a visitor. "Eddie is here and wants to talk. Dad and Mathews are also here." Ellie was instantly annoyed because she knew he probably wouldn't be helpful and he would just mutter threats at them, but she quickly grabbed her things out of the vehicle and followed Lauren inside to the family room and took a seat.

Of course she was correct in her assumption of the latest unwanted guest. Lauren began. "Eddie is here, and he is saying that Thomas was still able to communicate with him and that he is pissed and will find a way back to us if we don't stop speaking with the spirits and trying to find out information. He says he will cause problems for us and can manipulate our minds and alter moods. He says you are the funniest to get a hold of Mom."

Ellie jumped up without another word and started to walk out to the backyard to work on landscaping, and Lauren asked her, "Where are you going?"

Ellie was more than happy to tell Eddie she was too busy to listen to his shit. "I am not interested in listening to any more from him."

Lauren spouted out what was pouring out of Eddie. "He says he will cause us problems, just wait and see."

"I will take it as it comes, Eddie. And let me assure you this. Whether I am on this side or the other, I will personally make sure you are hunted down like a rabid dog and dealt with. So I am wishing you the best of luck." Ellie made sure to shut the door firmly behind her as she exited and made her way down to the other side of the stone wall by the house to pick up where she had left off thinning out her flowers. She was in no mood to deal with any evil threats and just wanted to get lost in her own thoughts.

Ellie hadn't been out there for ten minutes when Alexa ran out and said, "MiMi, come quick. Mommy needs you."

"Is your mommy having a seizure?"

"Uh huh."

Ellie popped up from the ground and went racing inside behind Alexa. There was Lauren, on the ground in full seizure mode, so Ellie calmly jumped into action and got her on her side because her face was smashed into the floor, making breathing hard. When her body would finally relax she could take a breath.

In her mind, Eddie was doing what he said he would do, and she had no doubt he was able to trigger the seizure, but she would never give him that credit aloud, and she went about the motions until Lauren slowly came to after three to four back-to-back seizures had taken hold of her body.

"Alexa, you did such a good job going and getting help for your mommy. MiMi is so proud of you." They all had been working with her on what to do if she sees her mother having a seizure and how to help her. After Lauren was coherent for a few minutes, she started to tell her mother what happened.

"After you went outside, Dad and Mathews tried to get Eddie to leave, and he wouldn't, so they went outside, and I was following them with Alexa when the seizure came on. They couldn't get back inside to me because Eddie threw up a barrier." Lucky for Lauren, the living wasn't affected by it, and Alexa was able to alert Ellie so she could help her daughter.

The Westons only had to put up with Eddie for another twenty-four hours when he let his guard down, following Ellie on one of her walks, and Eddie walked into a barrier that the chief, Jack, and Mathews had put up—like the one set for Thomas—that pushed him away for good. Lauren was more than happy to relay the news to her mother. "Dad says we only have two more partners to get rid of and then it will be easier to find items that they buried and have been protecting."

Ellie was so glad to hear that hopefully there was light at the end of the tunnel. After Lauren delivered the news, Ellie felt relief, but she was missing Jack terribly. She went upstairs and sat in his walk-in closet looking at the picture boards that were still sitting there from his service. She let the tears fall. She had been so busy with work and dealing with the farm and spirit world that it kind of numbed the pain of his loss, but it was always there and would forever be.

The next few days picked up again with visits from new spirits because one more partner was gone and that made them feel safe to speak and tell all they knew:

- Aola Callahan, age thirteen: She was sent to the farm by her father who was a partner and she spit in the face of a runner and was beheaded.

- Juliet Dubois, age nineteen: She was kidnapped in Paris, France by one of the partners, Saint Torrent. She was put in a three-by-nine crate with nine other girls, and she was the only one that survived the forty-seven-day journey to America. When she arrived, they put her to work in a garden, and one day she hit her bare foot with the tool and developed an infection and died a short time later. (The partners in Paris referred to the organization as "The Institute.")

- Ines, age tweve: Lived in the county. She was kidnapped and brought to the farm. She met other girls from abroad that were brought there. She was starved to death; the year was 1840.

- Isabella, age thirteen: She was kidnapped from her family out west. She was at the farm for two to three days when she was raped and her throat was slit.

- Gretta O'Reilly, age eight: She was kidnapped in Ireland and brought to the farm. She was considered "exotic" and treated very well at first. Then they started breaking her down. They first took away her clothes and then hairbrush and daily food. Then they started to make her work very hard. She was not supposed to be touched, but one day a runner raped her, and when they found him on top of her, he jumped up and used her as a human shield. they accidentally sliced her abdomen open, and her innards fell out, and she bled to death.

- Elanore, age twenty-one: She dated Hanson, also twenty-one. He was a partner, and his father was a partner. When she found out what kind of operation they had, she went to the sheriff in Stenson, who had her shot because he was also involved.

- Tillia, age nine: Came from France. She was being raised in a group home by a nice lady named Minnie. Every couple of months, "officers" would show up at her door saying they found homes for girls, and they would ship the girls to America to be brought to the farm. When she arrived, she was raped and starved, and she died one night because of a seizure…It was bitter cold.

- Augusta, age fourteen: She came from the county to the east, and her father raped and molested her and dropped her off at the farm. She made a friend, Summer, age sixteen. Summer was kidnapped from the county to the south. She had watched her entire family (mother, father, two older brothers, and baby sister) be burned alive in their home. Augusta and Summer were both raped and starved and eventually beaten and dragged by horses to their death. The year was 1826

- Tony Thorton: One of the partners, he was worse than Thomas. He too killed his own child. He went to Paris and acted as if he was a police officer so he could take orphan children and people from their homes to send to the farm.

- Serenity, age nine: Her father traded her at the farm for another girl..It was towards the end of the operating farm/orphanage. The raid happened six months later, and she was killed because the raiders thought she was a runner because she was dressed like a boy. She met Tony Thorton and said he acted like a girl, didn't like to get dirty. She thought he was probably gay.

- Darla, age twelve: The year was 1840. She was knocked out and kidnapped and brought to the farm. She didn't elaborate on what happened to her.

- Trinity, age fourteen: American Indian girl who was killed in the raid against her tribe. She thinks her brother may have survived the raid by climbing a tree and hiding.

- Indian boy, age eleven: Hadn't been named yet. He died the night of the raid against his tribe. He was stabbed to death as he was trying to get on his horse.

- Sarah, age fourteen: She was killed on the farm because she was able to read the organizations hand signs. A flat palm with the other hand rubbing a circle motion on it meant to round them up A flat palm with the other hand sliding two fingers up and down meant ready to fight. A flat palm being drummed with fingers meant Indians.

- Fern, age eleven: Indian girl. She was captured in the raid and brought back to the farm, where she was raped by many. They starved her for days and gave her water that had a foul smell, so she didn't drink it. One day they decided to break her body piece by piece; they started by breaking her pelvis, then smashed her toes. They took a mallet to her ankles. Then a man jumped up and down on her legs until they were shattered and then broke her arms next. Once they realized her back was broke and she couldn't feel the torture anymore, they snapped her neck.

Lauren warned her mother that their last visitor would be a rough one, as Jack had given a few details upfront to his daughter on what had happened to sweet young Fern. After Lauren had relayed all of Fern's story to her mother, Ellie thanked their young guest for being so brave and coming forward with her story and then let the tears roll down her face. Not much was said for a few minutes.

Finally Fern spoke up through Lauren and requested a bowl of cereal to eat, like the one Alexa had been enjoying. Ellie was more than happy to accommodate their new spirit friend and went about the task as if she were serving up one for a grandchild. "Which color bowl would she like?"

"Purple," replied Lauren, and Ellie delivered the bowl to the kitchen island so Fern could watch the animated program that was already on while she ate her fare. Even though Ellie herself couldn't see the young guest, it made her feel better to help make her existence on the other side a little better.

Ellie finished up her evening chores, grabbed a glass of wine, and went out to the front porch with her cell phone in hand to attend to some pressing work emails and then settle into her favorite word puzzle game app. A short time later, Lauren stepped out to catch some air, and before she went in she told her mother, "Dad says if you can stay out here for fifteen more minutes, they are going to use you again for a decoy." Ellie just gave a sly grin and quick nod, and Lauren went back inside to start the girls' baths.

The time seemed to pass quickly with her complete attention on the word puzzles that kept popping up on her phone, and when she glanced at the time, forty-five minutes had passed, so she thought it was time to get back inside. Ellie poked her head into the bathroom to ask Lauren if they had had any luck, and she was pleased with the response. "Yes, they got one of the bad guys, so they are just down to one or two more."

"Good. They will get the others soon." And with that thought, she exited the steamy room and headed upstairs to put on her sleeping attire, hopefully Alexa wouldn't be kept up all night by others, which made the night very short. Ellie finally plopped down on the couch and Alexa was already off to dreamland with the help of a natural sleep aid that was slipped into her sippy cup of juice. It didn't take long for Ellie to drift off to sleep and sleep hard, until the dream.

She wasn't sure if her uneasiness about the players that had to be dealt with conjured up the dream she had, or if someone jumped into her relaxed mind to give a subtle threat, but whatever the cause, she was jarred wide awake before 2:00 A.M…The dream started out with her, Jack, Lauren, and Alexa dealing with antics from the evil partners. The bad spirits were making the pets soil in the house time after time. Alexa was getting pushed around, and they were threatening to go after Lauren, and all the while the dream played out through a cell phone screen.

Then the dream ended but fired back up again with a blank cell phone screen and the image of a hallway, Ellie could hear Lauren screaming for her, and Jack was nowhere around. Then all of the sudden the screen turned a corner, and you could faintly make out Lauren farther back, and she was slightly bent forward with her hands out in front of her, bracing for something terrible coming her way, and she just kept saying "No! No! No! No!" and the dream ended as abruptly as it started.

Ellie sat up fast and had the creepiest feeling she was being sent a message and that the messenger was still in the family room with her. She quickly grabbed the remote and flipped on the news and just sat there trying to make sense of the dream that made no sense. Ellie was wide awake until 6:00 A.M. As the night slipped into dawn, the comfort of the morning light made her start to relax, and she fell back asleep and slept hard for another hour.

When Lauren came downstairs that morning, she fetched some juice out of the refrigerator and started telling her mother that she had the weirdest, most disturbing dream ever and that she didn't want to elaborate on it because it was so troubling. Ellie wasn't the only one that was sent a message last night. But from whom? One of the partners, but what was his name and what was his part in all of it? She was just hoping and praying it wasn't Thomas and that he hadn't found another exit hole from Hell.

Jack had told Lauren that he got word from the other spirits that the evil partners that were left were frustrated because the Westons quit talking on the farm and at their office building in town about their plan of attack and what they were working on to expose people and their terrible acts. They had been talking in code for a few weeks to avoid additional problems from the other side…And it was working.

The next spirit Jack, Mathews, and the chief bumped into was Frank Jorgen, a runner, and with no notice they were there in the family room one evening for a talk. Lauren went on to tell her mother about Frank and all that he had relayed. "He says he worked for Thomas for about a year. He needed a second job to help support his wife and two young children, a son and daughter. His job was to scout for young girls and kidnap them, but he never raped or murdered them.

"One day he didn't show up for work because his wife was very ill and needed help with the children. They only lived a mile south of the farm, and Thomas rode to their house with a couple of other runners. When he explained to Thomas why he hadn't shown up for work, Thomas shot his wife and the runners smothered his children. Then Thomas turned to him and asked him if he was ready to come to work now, and he said no so Thomas shot him. The year was 1848.

"He realized he was bringing those children to their deaths, and he prayed to God every night for forgiveness, so when he gave his life for his family, God spared his soul and allowed him to remain on the farm."

Jack quickly started to explain that now Frank was going to help them with gathering intel and battling the evil partners, whether he wanted to or not. Otherwise they were going to push him to the boundaries, and he would be forced to stay in heaven.

Ellie didn't like the idea and didn't like Frank's attitude through Lauren's interpretation. "I am not thrilled you are in my house because of what you did, so I assure you that you will be dealt with if you cross any of us!"

"Well it's not like I have a choice. Besides, you are going to need my help ridding the evil for quite some time…There were at least two other such farms operating in the country at that time—one out east and one further west." Ellie was sad to know that they had confirmation on that fact now because one young spirit boy had mentioned there were several buggies filled with boys from Kentucky that were loaded up to bring to work at the farm and that some of them went a different direction, which meant another location.

"Your husband is pretty clever." Ellie wasn't sure what the last remark that Frank threw out was about but had no doubt she would come to understand it down the road. She just agreed with his statement by nodding.

Lauren went on to relay more from Jack. "Dad says to leave the blanket on the futon alone because chief's mother is lying there and in the middle of "transitioning" from her spirit form. Indians have different beliefs; some believe in heaven and some believe their spirit takes another path through reincarnation and their final end."

"Her name is Rosalee, and it might take several days before she is transitioned into the next life." Ellie was somewhat fascinated at the idea of reincarnation but was also sad for the chief when he spoke up and said, "That will be the last I see of my mother. "

"I am sorry, Chief. Will that be your path eventually?"

"No, I have different beliefs. Mine is in heaven, but some of us choose another path when we die. No one really knows what happens after transitioning, and you take an animal life form, but it is our understanding it is not perpetual, but no one really knows."

Ellie just nodded and felt she should not ask any more questions because the chief was saddened by the event, and they were private people. The unexpected visit ended, and everyone settled into their routines for the evening.

By the end of the week, the Westons were all needing a break, so Ellie went to her sister Kelly's for the weekend. She had moved back to the area after Jack's passing so she could be closer to her family. Lauren and Leo decided to take advantage of Ellie being away for the evening and invited another young couple over for pizza, beer, and cards.

As the evening wore on and the card game ended, Lauren started getting a migraine, and her girlfriend suggested she try eating a gummy enhanced with THC. Lauren was told that marijuana was good for epilepsy, so she ate a couple that were offered to her and at first she didn't feel much, but within thirty minutes after eating them it was as if she was in a movie watching it play out around her in a loud surround-sound speaker system.

It was as if every nerve ending in her brain was given oxygen and caffeine and her sensory faculties were wide open. She could see a girl spirit of about thirteen with blonde hair standing in the family room with all of them, not saying anything to Lauren but showing her how the raid looked from the farm's view during the raid..

The girl jumped into Lauren's mind, giving her a front row seat to all that took place that night, but she was showing her the attack with daylight so Lauren could visually see all the chaos that took place. First came the loud gunfire and the smell of gunpowder. Then she could see fire along the river, hear the roaring and crackling of the fire, and smell the heavy smoke.

Next came the animals trying to flee the area, and they were running past her through the family room—dogs, horses, black rabbits, cows. They were frightened and trying to escape the brutality of Thomas's men. Then came people running and screaming towards the house, but they didn't come past the door.

Lauren kept asking her friend if she could see all that she was seeing, but her friend just laughed because she was high from ingesting a couple of gummies herself and thought Lauren was just hallucinating from being stoned. Little did her friend know that ingesting the THC just opened Lauren's mind up even more to the gift she had been given.

By the evening's end, Lauren was wrung out and ready for bed because the vivid images playing out for her were terrifying, loud, and exhausting, and she had been experiencing them for more than two hours.

After their company left, Leo put Lauren to bed and thought he better wait until the morning before he asked her too many questions. He was thankful that the girls were spending the night at his mother's house and they could sleep in. Lauren was going to need a little more rest from the busy evening.

When Ellie arrived home, Lauren told her about the experience she had had the night before. They both wondered who the girl was. Hopefully she would present herself to them soon and tell them who she was and what all she knew and saw. Ellie was amazed yet again that Lauren was blessed with such a gift, even though at times it seemed almost overwhelming to Lauren because there were always spirits around and new ones coming forward to speak to Lauren on a continual basis now.

The start of the week was busy, and Ellie couldn't believe they were into the month of September already and nearing the one year mark of Jack's passing. She also couldn't believe what all they had been through, what they had accomplished, and all they had yet to accomplish. Ellie was thankful Jack was with them the whole way and that their new extended family of spirit world was there to help. They all needed each other's strengths.

Lauren had been staying home with the girls and trying to work from home the last month. That decision helped save quite a bit in child care costs, and when they went down for naps, she was able to get a lot done, but she was also kept even more busy helping speak with new spirits that either came forward on their own with no warning or were found by Jack and his crew.

She was able to collect a lot of good information from them and relay it to her mother when she got home in the evenings, so they were able to amp up the stream of information, which was helping them get rid of the evil partners as quickly as they were showing up. Otherwise they could all be taken over by those that took so much from so many already…The Westons weren't going to allow that to happen.

Things were starting to shift; more spirit partners of the organization were starting to show up and hide in dens on the Weston's property across the creek, protecting the boxes that the Westons so desperately wanted to get their hands on because of all the valuable information in them that would help connect the dots to all those involved.

It was taking every good spirit to help keep an eye on things and report back to Jack, Mathews, and the chief. Unbeknownst to the evils and the living, Jack's crew had been going every night and doing a raid, and their new system was working. They were able to rid a couple of them every time, but they weren't telling Lauren and Ellie how they were able to do it, in order to protect their new plan of attack. It was best to keep it from all ears, even those on the good side, so that children spirits couldn't be tricked into relaying such information to the evils and so those hiding out in the Weston's home unde-tected wouldn't hear.

A young girl spirit that had witnessed a lot of the meetings in town in the Weston's building had been murdered there and was now staying at the farm. She was able to repeat their "creed" to Lauren for her to write it down and give it to Ellie:

"I pledge my loyalty to our government to where I am truthful to the brotherhood. Our brotherhood vows to protect our country and keep order in the people. We the people, for our people, for our country."

Ellie felt their whole "creed" was disgusting! Vowing to protect the coun-try? Keep order in the people? They were murdering, evil assholes. She could-n't believe how so many of them thought what they were doing was okay and that their right to do whatever was above the law . . . even God's.

One such partner was escorted to the Weston's house when he was cap-tured by Jack and Matthews after leaving the den. Jack had instructed Lauren to call her mother at work so they could speak with Alfonso; he was one of the overseas partners from Spain.

When Lauren got her mother on the phone Alfonso began speaking and Lauren repeated all that he said: "My name is Alfonso, and I was thirty-three years old and a partner when I was killed on my property in New York. I also owned property in California and many other places all over the world. I would lure girls to the dock and kidnap them and ship them here from Spain. There were many partners, and we are all aware of what you are trying to do, and we will be coming from all over the world to stop you."

Before he had said all that he did, Ellie had already been mulling it over in her mind and realized that it was an international ring. Alfonso kept speak-ing. "I killed many people, and I am not sorry for what I did. If we were oper-ating today with the technology that is available now, the operation would have been huge and unstoppable."

After the last conceited comment from Alfonso, Ellie had heard enough from him and said, "Alfonso, adios!" He was then ushered out and pushed over the edge into hell where he belonged. Ellie thought, *one more down and who knows how many more to go*. Only time would tell…

Lauren gave her attention back to her mother on the phone and shared with her, "Chief's mother has now completely vanished from the futon, which means that her transition is complete, so the chief is really sad right now.

"I'm sorry for the chief. They must have been close, and I know it's got to be hard on him. Let me know if there is anything we can do." Lauren said she would and ended the call. Ellie thought maybe she should swing by the local florist and pick up some flowers to bring to the chief and his family. She was at a loss of what to do for them . . . except pray.

When Ellie arrived home, the house was busy with little ones running around and screeching about, but that would end soon in the next two to three weeks with Lauren's completed new home, and Ellie would miss some of those moments. Once the girls were in the highchairs and quieted by cartoons and dinner, she was able to speak with Jack and Mathews there in the kitchen.

"So, what have you guys been up to since we last spoke?"

Both of them let on that there wasn't much new to report, and then Mathews starting chuckling and Jack asked him what was so amusing.

"I was just remembering the first time we met. I was sitting on the big boulder down by the spring, and it was only a couple of days after you passed and you were running around beating and yelling on the dome like they could here you."

Jack chimed in. "Well I didn't know how to get their attention and I was trying everything I could. It was like looking into a giant snow globe and no one could hear or see me." They all laughed at the thought of poor Jack trying to reach his family, in a panic, but there they all were, communicating and being a family.

Ellie was curious how he had worked past that invisible barrier between the living and spirit world. "Jack, how did you make it through to us finally?"

Jack answered her, "It just took time."

"Well how did you know to do the hand signal?"

"It just came to me." There was still so much to learn about the other side of life and how everything worked in the spirit world.

Then Mathews turned his comments to Ellie. "I would be sitting there on the same boulder and watch you pick up sticks and try and pull weeds out of the spring, and you would sink in the muck almost a foot and would have trouble puling yourself out. In fact, a couple of times you fell in the spring."

They all laughed at that, especially Ellie, because she could just imagine herself struggling and getting irritated that the sludge was holding her captive, and she always had plenty of outside work to do, and that was just slowing her down.

The conversation wound down, and Ellie got busy making the evening coffee and throwing something in the oven. She loved to go to sleep with the aroma of something freshly baked in the air, whether it was a savory bread or something sinfully sweet. She figured everybody loved the good smells and enjoyed eating the fresh-baked surprises, especially since most of the spirits were starved while they were living.

Lauren poked her head back into the kitchen as her mother was finishing up. "Hey, I wrote down the three answers in the notebook to the questions that Uncle Grant asked Grandpa to answer."

"Thanks, sweetie." Ellie had forgotten all about that. The last time Jack had made a trip to heaven, he had made it a point to hunt down Ellie's father and get the answers.

Ellie wiped the dish soap off her hands, went over to the notebook, and opened it up and read the answers. Then she gave Grant a quick text. It only took him five minutes for him to text her back, and his response was

"Wow! That is crazy. I will call you in a few days after I get home from this job site."

Ellie shot him back the thumbs up and smiley face emojis. She figured he was in shock, but when he was on those commercial installation sites for his job, he didn't have much time to communicate with family. Grant worked for a large supplier that handles everything from HVAC to organized storage systems for commercial buildings and multi-level apartment buildings and such.

The next three weeks were filled with final wedding preparations and finishing up loose ends on Lauren and Leo's new house. Their special day was set for September 28th. Ellie and Lauren were not only busy picking out flowers at Patty Clark's florist shop and ordering tables and linens to be delivered; they also went shopping for some clothes for some of the spirit girls and women. Everyone was excited about the upcoming wedding. Most of them on the other side hadn't seen a big wedding before, and they were all looking forward to it.

Lauren had decided to get married behind the barn in front of the big old apple tree that stood about thirty feet tall and was just as round. The tree sat behind the barn and in front of the spring. It was the perfect spot.

Ellie had hired one of her past clients that had managed a farm out east, and he had a lot of experiencing pruning fruit trees. So when he got done with the tree, it was nothing short of spectacular, and the the wood line behind it was also tended to make it a picture-perfect backdrop.

By the third week in September, everything was shaping up to be the perfect wedding. Lauren had asked her brother Chance if he would walk her down the aisle, and he agreed. It was going to be a hard day for all of them because Jack wasn't there beside them for everyone to see, but he would be there.

· It had been pretty quiet in the spirit world until a new partner showed up to start in with his antics, and he started by coming forward to speak. This guy had very special powers. Even Jack and Mathews couldn't push him over the edge or make him leave the house one night when he showed up and started with his threats.

Lauren was tending to Alexa in the family room, and she stopped what she was doing. "Mom, Dad and Mathews are here, and so is Thurman Wells. He was a partner, and he is saying it will be a wedding no one will ever forget."

That was enough to send Ellie over the edge, so she addressed Jack. "You need to make him leave now!" Lauren relayed her father's response.

"Mom, they have tried but they can't physically, and he won't leave."

Ellie addressed their latest trespasser directly. "Get out of my house you sack of shit!"

Their unwanted guest just laughed, and as quickly as he appeared...he disappeared.

"Well, he is going to try to be a problem. Don't worry, Lauren. I'm sure Dad and Mathews will figure out how to deal with him, and all will be fine."

Lauren hesitantly said, "I hope so," and everyone was certainly thinking that. Thurman Wells tried making things difficult that week. Lauren suffered several seizures, and one occurred just as she pulled out of the drive, with Alexa in the backseat. She was lucky. Her vehicle ran off the road into their lower bean field before she got to the concrete bridge and creek bed. When Ellie heard Lauren's SUV's horn make a repetitive beeping sound, she looked out the window to see Lauren in the field hitting the steering wheel with her head in a back and forth motion because of the seizure.

Ellie went running down the hill, and at about that, time Leo pulled up. He had been next door working on finishing touches on their house when he heard the commotion. Ellie opened the vehicle door, and Lauren's seizure had stopped, and she was in a semi-conscious state, and Alexa was in the back seat quietly whimpering over what had taken place.

It didn't take Lauren too long to come around. With some of her seizures she could be completely unresponsive for over an hour. Leo told her that whatever running needed to be done, he would do it or drive her but that she couldn't drive for a few days. Lauren didn't object and knew how lucky they were that the seizure hadn't started a few seconds later. The outcome could have been different.

Ellie wasn't sure what else Mr. Wells had planned, but she was hoping he was overstating his abilities. But she also understood he was a new, unknown entity on the dark side of spirit world that brought too many questions as to what he was capable of.

The next few days were fairly uneventful, and Ellie let everything go. They would just deal with whatever came their way, and she would keep praying to God. She finished up her week at work and managed to help Lauren with all that comes with hosting a big wedding, and everyone was feeling good about what had gotten accomplished, with just a few odds and ends to go.

The forecast for the next ten days looked good. The next few days were going to be cooler than normal for that time of year, but it would be warming back up by the start of the next week. There was no rain in the forecast, but given it was hurricane season in the south, and the time of year, precipitation could easily become a nuisance, especially since the ceremony was to be held outdoors. But the barn was all decked out and ready for the celebration no matter what the weather did.

Ellie was thankful she didn't have to work the coming weekend and was looking forward to doing some personal things she enjoyed in between all the goings on. She went to sleep that Friday evening feeling the most optimistic and at peace with her life than she had since Jack's passing. When Ellie woke up the next day, it was a beautiful Saturday morning with an unseasonable chill in the air, which was perfect for hiking. So after Ellie finished her morning chores, she grabbed her gun and threw on her boots and walked out on the side porch where Red was already waiting…They both enjoyed these walks. It let Ellie decompress and also provided decent exercise climbing those steep hills in the woods. She still liked to stay in shape, and it was good for her arthritic back to maintain the muscles in her legs.

As they started up the first big hill behind the barn, Ellie remembered that she hadn't grabbed her cell phone. Her children wanted her to carry it on her walks for an emergency, even though she kept it on silent so she wouldn't be disturbed during the only time she took for herself. She didn't like that uneasy feeling that her sixth sense was giving her, but she didn't want to bother going back to the farmhouse, and brushed it off to her heightened sense because of all that they had gone through in the last several months.She was anxious to get on the path and get lost in her thoughts. Red was already way ahead chasing squirrels up trees.

The old logging road she used for her hiking path was a little overgrown because she hadn't used it during the summer months this year. There were many other things that had taken her time and energy lately. Normally, with her and Red utilizing the path, it would keep the undergrowth knocked down pretty good.

When she made it to the top of the ridge, she could see a couple hundred feet ahead, and there was the giant beech tree that she loved lying on its side with a giant ball of earth and stones attached to the end of the tree trunk. As Ellie got within twenty feet of it, she could see about a five-foot-deep divot where the root system had been, she thought it must have pulled up with all the rain that they had during the first part of spring.

She only made it ten more steps when the leaves below her feet gave way, and she felt herself falling down a tight, three-foot-wide hole until she hit a sandstone ledge. Ellie knew she was hurt pretty bad. Her right leg below her knee was causing excruciating pain, and the left side of her abdomen felt like it was on fire with hot fluid running down it.

She had fractured her leg, and a piece of jagged rock had pierced her side, and she could feel the blood escaping from the wound. As she sat there in the tight space, she was trying to get her senses. She could her Red off in the distance, still barking and chasing squirrels, and when she glanced up, she could see daylight and guessed she had fallen about fifteen feet into the hole. Out of habit, Ellie reached into her coat pocket for her cell phone and realized the terrible mistake she had made by not going back for it.

As she sat there trying to assess her situation, she could feel the cool dampness of the earth around her forming a cloak, and she could smell its musty nature, making her feel uneasy and claustrophobic.

Panic started to set in as she felt herself slipping into unconsciousness while thinking that her children had already suffered a terrible loss just a few months before, and now…

When Ellie glanced back up to the top, she was surprised to see someone looking down at her. She recognized the face only by description…With as much energy as she had left, she muttered, "Mathews?" The last thing she heard was a concerned and comforting voice. "Ellie!"

About the Author

B. West lives in a small community in southern Indiana and has sold real estate for more than twenty-five years. She is blessed to live on a beautiful farm that holds many memories. She has two children and three grandchildren, all of whom she adores. She looks forward to watching her grandchildren grow up to find as much happiness and joy in their lives as they can.

"Because of you I am Free"

- ANDREWS